LEONARD SMITH

Written By: AJ Harrison

First Edition Copyright© 2016 by Austin Harrison
Pen Legacy Publishing
Philadelphia, PA
Edited by: Summer Fitch
Design and Layout by: Junnita Jackson

Pen Legacy books may be purchased for educational, business, or sales promotional use. For information please e-mail the special Markets Department at
lovetherealyou0510@gmail.com.

First Edition
Library of Congress Catalog: 2016940949
Paperback ISBN: 978-099618805-0

Dedication

This book is dedicated to my loving and supportive wife Aleshia (Buttercup). She has been my inspiration and motivation during our time together. My mom Judy Harrison, who has supported me during all of my difficult times. You both are the reason I was able to finish this book. Your unconditional love has carried me to where I'm at right now. I am forever indebted to both of you and love you both more than words can express.

Acknowledgements

I thank all of my friends and family. I consider my frat brothers of Phi Beta Sigma Lambda Upsilon Chapter my family. Many of these brothers have been with me throughout all of the ups and downs. Your unconditional support has meant the world to me. The funny and deep conversations over the past twenty years have been some of the most enlightening and hilarious conversations never recorded.

I appreciate all of the people I grew up with in Penllyn and Ambler. There were great times back in the 80's and 90's and you all have supported me in my entire social and business ventures over the years. I love you guys and will always be connected to my hometown.

There are too many frat, friends and family and business mentors to name everybody by name but each one of you mean the world to me and helped me become a better man.

And finally to Summer Fitch (editor) & Charron Monaye (Pen Legacy Publishing), thank you both so much for providing me with this opportunity to become an author. This has always been a dream of mine and you two manifested my thoughts and brought them to life on paper. Looking forward to creating a publishing dynasty together!

Contact Information

Ajh295@gmail.com All correspondence can be sent to that email. Book information can be viewed and purchased at www.PenLegacy.com

Chapter 1
Patton,

It's so cold! You can never get warm behind these walls; with a blanket designed more for an elementary school kid to sleep with and a thin jumpsuit as a daily outfit, warmth was always at a premium. You always felt like you could see your breath on a cold winter's day. Sometimes the outside in the winter looked and felt warmer than the inside. Aside from the cold temperature, there is no warmth in this place. The residents are steely and life isn't guaranteed to anyone. A wrong look or stare could get you killed in an instant. In 1983 this place was hell on earth. No human being would ever sign up for this type of life, much less a teenager. There are strong adult men in here ranging in ages from 17 to 90 years old and all with a stories that defy belief. Waking up here on a daily basis doesn't elicit any hope for the future and really has men question their existence. This was no place for anyone, much less someone that was not fully developed mentally, emotionally, or physically. This place is Patton State Penitentiary (PSP) 45 miles north of San Francisco, California. PSP is unforgiving and unfeeling; just to make sure you and other prisoners like you never make it out or come back for any reason.

This institution housed some of the worst criminals in the state of California. Many men here were doing life sentences for violent crimes. Many had no remorse for their crimes and no regard for human life. The meaning of life and humanity had seemingly escaped these prisoners and daily survival inside the walls of PSP was all they were concerned with. In 1983, the homicide rate at PSP was the highest out all of the state correctional facilities and many inmates rallied for reform due to the unsafe conditions. Hardened lifers had a difficult time existing in PSP, so imagine how a 155 pound 17 year old felt? He was scared but he couldn't let anyone see it. To show weakness in PSP was a recipe for disaster. A scared man would be eaten alive in this concrete jungle. At night you cry into your pillow so no one hears you. You put on the toughest face you can and pray that you don't get jumped or assaulted by multiple inmates.

For the first time in his life, Leonard was scared. Entering PSP was a tumultuous experience for Leonard. The environment was much different from the youth detention center in Oakland and the Santa Rita County lockup. PSP was a cold place. You could feel the tension as soon as you walked in. This wasn't a place where people fucked around. This was life or death. Leonard was dying on the inside but put a brave face on as he was led into the intake center. His mind was racing. (The counselors at the Oakwood Detention Center tried to get Leonard mentally prepared for this moment. They let him know that shit was different at PSP. They told him that there were killers at PSP. Oakwood was full of emotional boys but few killers. Some turned out to be killers but most were delinquent emotional boys). When the gate shut behind him, Leonard knew his life would never be the same. As he entered he was cuffed with his wrists in front of him and was in line with 20 other new inmates. There were no inspirational posters on the wall like at Oakwood. There were no group meetings being held or homework tutors. The walls were gray concrete and the paint was chipping all over. The floor was hard and offered no support. It felt like there hadn't been heat on in years. The guards were massively built, armed with loaded 9mm handguns and never repeated what they said. The new inmates were un-cuffed one at a time and told to strip naked. Their clothes were put in a green trash bag and labeled with the prisoner's name on it. Leonard watched as his new fellow inmates were treated like members of a concentration camp. It seemed inhumane to Leonard that grown men had to strip naked and be on display in front of strangers and the horror show had truly just begun; it was Leonard's turn to get strip searched.

"Smith, do you have any weapons?" The guard yelled.

"No." Leonard said with certainty.

"Tongue out and move it side to side and cough. Bend over and spread your cheeks. Ok, cough again!" The guard said with force.

"I heard you like to knockout old ladies. I'm reading your rap sheet, you a punk mother-fucker! Aggravated assault and robbery, huh? Ain't no old ladies or young punks here. Your ass is in here with killers so a young punk bitch like you ain't got nowhere to hide. These cats don't like a young punk like you hitting on old ladies. You gonna be crying like a pussy before long." Leonard didn't say anything and looked straight ahead.

*Leonard was given two folded prison jumpsuits. The jumpsuits were a faded pale green color. They were called jumpsuits but they were a short sleeve top and khaki type bottoms. They were almost paper thin with **PSP** stitched on the back.*

"Here is your prison outfit. You can never be in PSP without your outfit on. Being without a PSP issued outfit equals a week in the hole."

Leonard was given a Ziploc bag with a plastic toothbrush, a bar of soap, and a small tube of toothpaste. He was also given two pairs of socks, 2 T-shirts, and 2 pairs of underwear. A sandpaper-like washrag and towel were also given to him and he was told to stand back in line. As he got back in line his hands were once again cuffed in front of him. Leonard had his mean face on but was dying and crying on the inside. It took everything in him not to allow the tears to stream down his face. Mentally he had to be strong but emotionally he was fractured. His teenage life was now over. On the street he acted like a grown man and now he was among nothing *but* grown men and this is when shit got real. These were not just grown men but adult socio and psychopaths. No amount of time spent in a juvenile facility could prepare Leonard for the anxiety he now experienced. Survival was his new reality. If he wanted any type of future in his 20's, he would have to learn how to survive. There wasn't anyone here to help him. The prison guards were only concerned with ensuring that there were no incidents happening on their watch. How an inmate feels was the last issue they were concerned with. Leonard had to rely on every fiber of his being to make it to the age of 18. For Leonard, it was now a possibility that he may be faced with employing the old adage - kill or be killed.

He was walked down to E pod cell 12; because he was new and a teenager he was housed in a unit that allowed him to be alone in his cell Leonard was placed on 72-hour suicide watch, which meant guards would check on his cell every 15 minutes. Leonard lie on the cot in his 6 by 8 cell and thought about all the decisions he made that led him to this undesirable existence. He spent a large portion of his teenage years in various youth detention centers in Oakland, however this was different. There were no guest speakers or unit counselors. There were no day visits from family and friends. There was no homework to complete or school assignments to do. All Leonard had was his thoughts and his desire to survive. He was sentenced to -5-15 years for battery and aggravated assault and because his juvenile rap sheet was so long, he was sentenced as an adult. So here he was, 17 and among the most violent criminals in the state of California. There was no way out and he wasn't eligible for parole until he served at least 54 months. Even then, parole was not guaranteed and only model inmates or inmates with lesser charges received parole.

The first night in PSP as Leonard lay alone in his cell he began to think about all of the horrible choices he made.

"Why did I hit Patty? I should've listened to my sister and went to school. What the fuck have I been thinking about? What the fuck did I do to my life?" Before now Leonard never pondered his existence. His only concern on the streets was being a menace to society. On the streets he was a wolf not a sheep and he made sure that everyone knew he was a problem. Many days he sat in the youth detention center and listened to guest speakers come in and warn the juvenile boys of the dangers of the streets and if they continued to make bad decisions, they would end up in a place like PSP. Leonard was the type that never took any of the speakers serious and laughed at the stories with little regard for any of the consequences of his actions.

Now as Leonard lay on his hard cot he thought back to the guest speakers at the detention center. He thought about all of the words of wisdom that were given to him throughout his seventeen years of existence and he just didn't know what to do now. Grown men with no regard for human life were now occupying his personal space and there was no down time at PSP. Every movement throughout PSP was gauged and clocked by fellow inmates and guards. Leonard would have to find out how to survive for at least the next five years. There was no safe haven for any inmate, much less a seventeen year old.

"I will never come back to this place!" Leonard repeated this to himself through the night just low enough that no other inmate could hear him. That night, Leonard cried in his pillow until 5:00 in the morning.

At 5:30 am the entire unit was woken up and lined up outside their cells for morning headcount. Each inmate would step forward and announce their inmate number. Once they did that, they would step back and lineup in single file for the mess hall. A guard stood at each end of the line and Leonard's heart pounded as he tried to brace himself for the unexpected. He looked straight ahead focusing on the back of the head of the guy in front of him so as not to seem moved by his first encounter. Everybody on the unit knew he was the new guy. Some guys whistled as he walked by. Others yelled at him and blew him kisses. Unfortunately, teenage boys were like pretty women at PSP.

"That's the new cat from East Oakland." "Look at this mother fucker, he already think he bad. This ain't the detention center bitch." All the guards laughed.

These were just some of the things yelled out to Leonard as he made his way to the mess hall. It felt like the longest walk ever from his cell to the mess hall. Breakfast, or *mush shit* as the inmates called it, was made up of dry hardened oatmeal and even drier biscuits. Leonard got his tray and looked for a table as he went to sit down and a 6'5" 245lb lifer named Bone got in his way. (Leonard was 6'1, lanky, and weighed 159 pounds soaking wet. He had a decision to make; think about being a model inmate and hopefully get released in four years, or defend his manhood and get some PSP respect). Leonard didn't say excuse me, walked past the dude, and put his tray down. All eyes in the mess hall were trained on Leonard and Bone. Bone's reputation at Patton was that of a bully and an inmate rapist. Everybody at Patton was scared of

Bone. Leonard was scared of him as well. Leonard thought about Arlene and Marvin and the rage built up inside of him. He began to look past Bone and could only see his survival. He was either going to be a man or a bitch within the next 2 minutes. Dead or alive, Leonard was either going to gain much needed respect or be eaten by the sharks!

Bone said "Little nigga who you walking past?" Leonard didn't say anything. At that moment Leonard would change the course of his life In PSP. He stood in front of Bone, said nothing, and hit him with a left cross to the body and a right hook to the temple. Bone was knocked unconscious and his head was cracked on the concrete as he landed. The other inmates stood in shock. They couldn't believe what they just saw. Bone had terrorized new inmates in PSP for years; he was one of the most feared men in the California Prison system. Bone's defeat by Leonard was amazing for everyone watching - including the guards. Leonard just earned his respect at PSP and he was only 17 years old. Taking a stand and knocking out the most feared man in PSP ensured that no one would fuck with him during his stint. Leonard knew the prison code and had just shown that he was worthy of being looked at as a man. This was the only way for new inmates to get respect. The mess hall was buzzing and the inmates were yelling and jumping up and down. Many sat there with relief and disbelief. A high percentage of the inmates were terrorized by Bone and the vision of Bone bleeding and lying on the ground was a sign of a new day. During this interaction one man was intently observing Leonard's every move and it wasn't a guard.

Leonard's newfound respect caused him to reminisce on some of the boxing he learned six years ago. Leonard boxed as a pre-teen up to the age of 13. He unfortunately moved away from boxing, as his life of crime took precedence in his teenage years. At the age of 11 Leonard was in the gym and had hopes of making it to the golden glove championships one day. He displayed promise at the young age of 11 and his trainer knew he had potential but also knew that the Leonard had one foot in the street and one in the gym. The only reason Leonard was at the gym was because he kept getting in fights and the teacher at his school took him there to release some stress. At the time (1988) Mike Tyson was the Heavyweight Champion of the World and had worldwide recognition and adoration. Leonard was aware of how great Tyson was but at the time didn't have the maturity level to understand the impact boxing could have on his life. Leonard fought a few amateur fights, but by the time he was 13, it was clear that he chose the streets to display his fighting prowess.

Luckily for Leonard, no guard paid attention to this fight and Leonard wouldn't have to face any punishment. In fact, the guards were waiting for someone to knock the shit out of Bone. From here on out Leonard, may never have to face any more tests of his will; but danger was imminent everyday no matter what. Gangs were a reality in PSP and inmates joined mostly for protection. Each entity disguised as a gang was covertly designed to provide protection and a front for illegal activity in PSP. Leonard wasn't sure which faction he would choose but he had become aware that potential trouble existed either way. If he chose to stay to himself then he would be a target. If he joined a faction he may be involved in activities that threatened his parole in five years. Leonard simply wanted to survive and get out. But survival could mean death to someone else. This was not a game and Leonard knew that he had to be respected and also give it.

Chapter 2
Heavy Bag,

"I saw you in the mess hall. You have talent and I can tell that you boxed before. You threw a left cross and a straight right, which was very sharp. Those punches were precise and I see you've had some amateur experience. It takes a lot of heart to stand up to that nut case. That dude always intimidates the new guys but you didn't back down and showed what you're made of. I've been here for 15 years and this isn't the first time I've seen a young boy fight but this is the first time I've seen a combination like that."

Conrad Burrell *(CB is what he's been called since birth)* was doing life without the possibility of parole. He was born and raised in South Central Los Angeles. He was a seasoned member of the PSP community. A lifer in PSP can offer perspective on life and survival like no one else at PSP. CB was dark-skinned with seemingly yellow eyes and a bald head. He bared resemblance to the singer and actor Isaac Hayes. *Old head*, as he was affectionately called, had piercing eyeballs and was a super intense man. His presence demanded respect and although he was reformed, he would still do whatever was necessary to survive and exist. CB had the respect of every inmate at PSP and his existence was about as good as it could get at PSP. He had a single cell with a 13inch black and white in it so he was able to watch the fights, which he loved so much. His life revolved around boxing both in and out of PSP. In 1983 (when the boxing team started at PSP) Larry Holmes was the heavyweight champ, Marvin Hagler was the Middleweight champ; Thomas Hearns and Roberto Duran were both in the 147 – 150 mix. Aaron Pryor and Alexis Arguello just had 2 classic bouts and Ray "Boom Boom" Mancini was a star in the lightweight division. "Boom Boom" was the pride of Youngstown, Ohio and CB loved his heart and fighting spirit. Sugar Ray Leonard was boxing's biggest star at the time but was retired due to an eye injury. In '83 the only fight real boxing fans wanted to see was Sugar Ray vs. Marvin Hagler. CB stayed up many a night dreaming of watching that fight.

The days when the fights were on television were the best days of CB's life. He would settle in his cell with his snack food and a beverage and would be super excited. Since he had a single cell he didn't have to worry about sharing his space & could enjoy his love of the fights. Boxing was his passion and had been since he was 12 years old. CB was 12 in 1960, the same year that Cassius Clay (later known as Muhammad Ali) won the gold medal at the Olympics. He fell in love with boxing after watching Ali box in the Olympics and at that moment he knew what he wanted to do with his life. When Ali won the Heavyweight title 4 years later, CB was boxing as an amateur and he mimicked all of Ali's moves and style. CB would even try and write poems to be like Ali. He was a good young boxer with a lot of potential in the mid to early 60's.

At this juncture CB knew he was never getting out of PSP due to a double murder at the age of 18. His mission was to help the young bucks coming into PSP to try and get on the right track, leave PSP, and never return. Due to his background, CB naturally gravitated to leading the newly formed boxing team. He was always on the lookout for new talent and was keenly observing Leonard in the mess hall a few days ago.

"I boxed for a couple of years when I was 11-12 but then the streets took over. I thought about it when I was in juvy but never went back to it." Leonard explained.

"Shit happens," said CB.

"If you want to get back into boxing I can help" CB exclaimed.

"I didn't know PSP had a boxing team? No one told me that in intake. They just gave me some clothes and walked me to the cell".

"PSP isn't known for its hospitality. " CB said with a chuckle.

"PSP is going to be real tough for you without something to do to keep your mind off of the daily bullshit. Boxing has helped many men stay away from the gang shit but you have to be dedicated to the process. It won't be easy and we don't have the best equipment. We have a ring, speed bag, some jump ropes, weights and the heavy bag. That heavy bag can be used to take out all the frustrations you have. Got it? Listen, there are two rules for the boxing team; there is no fighting outside of the team and no quitting during a match. Boxing is 90% mental and 10% physical."

"I'm ready."

CB looked in Leonard's eyes and said, "The mental part comes in like Ali-Frazier 3, The Thrilla in Manilla; both of those guys were tested mentally for 14 rounds. Can you handle that?"

"I heard about that fight Back in Oakland but I never watched much TV. I remember seeing Ali fight Frazier 3 on channel 9. That was a tough fight and I was rooting for Frazier because he was the underdog." Leonard recollected.

CB continued, "That was a real fight but I'm going to show you some defense. The key to boxing is to hit and not get hit; Ali and Frazier were trading punches but not ducking punches. I respect both of them for the way they fought but the key is to avoid punches and not run into them."

"It's been 6 years since I've put on boxing gloves. I've been knocking cats out with my bare hands. Shit in the street has nothing to do with boxing. I never thought about boxing again, but maybe now is the time to get back in the game." Leonard looked down and muttered, "I'm trying to get out of here in '93. This shit is for the birds, but ain't nowhere I can go for a while, so I need to stay occupied."

CB smirked, "At least you can get out. Man I'm here until I die. No one to blame but me, but PSP ain't where I wanted to live or end my life. We all make decisions and I accept that; this is why I want you young cats to take heed and get your shit straight."

"CB I can't come back here ever!" Leonard quickly responded.

"Well Leonard, training starts tomorrow. I'm not fucking with quitters so go back to your cell and get your mind right. Decide of you want to turn your life around. Make a decision about how you want to spend the next five years. This won't be easy so you're going to have to dig deep and find out where your heart and mind is. Boxing can keep you busy in PSP but you will have to dedicate yourself. I can give you all the wisdom I have but the decision to excel is up to you."

"CB, I'm on it." Leonard vowed.

Leonard went back to his cell excited and scared at the same time. He was excited about getting back into boxing but scared to commit. The only thing he had committed to the past five years was the streets of East Oakland. Lying on the cot in his cell was the best place for him to get his thoughts together. In the gym back in Oakland he remembered seeing a fight poster for Marvin Hagler versus Bobby Watts in 1976. The guy running the gym was from Philadelphia, and he loved all the Philly fighters. They fought in South Philly at the spectrum and Watts beat Hagler by majority decision. Hagler was the undisputed Welterweight Champion of the World for 7 years. Leonard couldn't even think that far ahead, all he could think of was going back to the gym and getting all he training he could from CB.

The Heavy Bag is where it all started; combinations thrown, technique developed, and frustration let out. Heavy bag, heavy bag, heavy bag was all that was going through Leonard's head. The heavy bag is how Leonard would survive in PSP and stay out of anymore shit. For once in his life, Leonard felt like he had a purpose. He always felt angry and mad for having drug addicted and alcoholic parents growing up in the projects of East Oakland. Leonard was regrettably at PSP but finally after 17 years of fucking up, he had a reason to do right.

Leonard started doing pushups in his cell. The first night he could only do 8 pushups. Prior to getting locked up at PSP Leonard drank beer & alcohol and also smoked a lot weed and cigarettes. His body needed cleansing before he could be effective in training. Boxing training required a lot of stamina. A healthy lifestyle would be necessary if Leonard wanted to be serious about boxing. That night was the night Leonard decided that his mind, body, and soul would have to change. Success in boxing required discipline and up to this point Leonard didn't have any. He told himself that at 5:30am. He skipped breakfast and made his way to the boxing area. It couldn't be considered a boxing gym due to the size but it was the best he could get. It looked and felt more like a dusty dungeon as opposed to a boxing gym. The heavy bag looked like it could fall from the ceiling with a hard punch but CB assured all of his boxers that it was good to go. The ring had 2 loosely fitting ropes instead of the standard 3 that surround an official boxing ring. When you skipped rope some dust would fly up and the wooden floor would creak. This dungeon is where CB spent all of his time (when the fights weren't on). The focal point of the dungeon was a fight poster from The Thrilla in Manilla, which was the third fight between Muhammad Ali and Joe Frazier. Joe Frazier (when he was visiting Oakland) heard about the boxing team being formed in PSP and donated the fight poster. It was CB's prize possession and no one could touch it. There were also some pictures of CB an amateur and also some cut outs from Sports Illustrated and Ring Magazine. Ali, Hearns, Aaron Pryor, Sugar Ray Leonard, Joe Frazier and Larry Holmes were part of the collage. Although the dungeon wasn't the fanciest of places it was all boxing all day. The place emanated boxing.

"When do we hit the heavy bag?" Leonard asked CB.

"Soon son, soon" replied CB. First we have to get your mind right. I need you to think like a boxer and not a street dude anymore. It's hard to get the streets out of your blood. I've been here since '66 and I can still taste the streets. It's like a crooked bitch with good pussy. You know she ain't good for you but it's hard to leave her. One day you'll be back on those streets and the goal is not to come back here ever. In order for that to happen, you have to train your mind just like you train your body. Boxing can be your salvation but it's going to take hard work. 90% of the dudes in here ain't about shit and never will be. The ones on the boxing team have discipline but none of them are getting out. They're all doing life. Right now you're the only hope. So listen carefully and develop a philosophy that will enable you to thrive in PSP and on the outside. Keep skipping that rope and then we'll work on some technique." From 6:00 am until lunchtime CB and Leonard worked in the dungeon. Leonard learned to throw a left hook and how to duck a punch. He learned where to place his feet based on the style of fighter he was matched against. He did pushups until it felt like his arms would fall off. He skipped rope until his legs felt like wet noodles.

At lunch Leonard sat with CB and the other boxers. They talked boxing and diet. It was hard to eat right at PSP but CB had some pull in the kitchen and the boxing team was able to get a bit of a different diet. Plus, the warden was a big boxing fan so he always gave CB what he needed to make the boxing team productive. The inmates respected the boxing team and gained pride when they fought other prisons. No one had an issue with the boxing team receiving some extra vegetables and fruit. CB told Leonard that it was strictly water (no juice or soda) for the next 90 days during training. Leonard's first fight was in 3 months and CB was strict with what the boxers ate and drank. PSP, like many other state prisons, had a commissary area where inmates could purchase snack foods and juices. PSP also had a drug problem and many inmates were hooked on heroin and cocaine. The problem was so bad PSP was on the verge of banning all conjugal visits. CB banned all boxers from the commissary during training. Leonard loved sweets and juices. He had no diet out on the streets but remained lean because he played a lot of stickball and roughhouse basketball in East Oakland. Leonard would obey the wishes of CB. Conrad was the boxing trainer and the 1st man that Leonard ever looked up to. He respected the process and wanted to give it 100%.

After lunch Leonard still wanted to hit the heavy bag. He was itching to let out the aggression but CB still wouldn't let it happen. Leonard spent afternoons running out in the yard. He enjoyed the running although his stamina wasn't up to par and he lagged behind the rest of the team but didn't quit. After running in the yard they went back to the dungeon and CB put Leonard on the scale. 159 pounds is what Leonard weighed. He wasn't fat; but based on his height of 6'1" CB wanted him to fight at the welterweight limit of 150. The PSP boxing team had 2 heavyweights, 1 welterweight and 1 lightweight. CB wanted a welterweight on his boxing team since he admired that size fighter; Sugar Ray Leonard being his favorite. From the time CB saw Leonard knock out Bone in the mess hall he started sizing him up to be the welterweight champ at PSP. Because Leonard was raw, CB knew that it would take time for him to develop. Fighting on the amateur level is much different from a pro style. Amateur boxing is judged upon the amount of punches not for the impact. The PA boxing system judges fights with the same criteria of professional boxing. Conrad was constantly thinking about all of the nuances of boxing and at the same time all Leonard wanted to do was hit the heavy bag. CB had to remind himself that Leonard had potential but was only a few weeks shy of 18. Technically he was not even an adult yet but was knocking out grown men on the street and in PSP - this excited CB.

CB told Leonard that he wanted him to be a welterweight and he was fine with that. Leonard knew he could make the weight. CB also told Leonard that he couldn't hit the heavy bag until he weighed 150 pounds. He had to lose 9 pounds to get to the heavy bag. Leonard had a strong desire to hit that heavy bag and now knew what he had to do to reach his goal. He asked CB how long it would take to lose 9 pounds and CB told him typically 2 weeks. However Leonard was only 17 and 9 pounds was nothing to lose. For two weeks, Leonard ran 4 miles in the yard each day. He also jumped rope, did push-ups and sit-ups to go with the running. CB wouldn't let him put on gloves until he got down to 150. That meant that Leonard would go in the gym and watch his PSP teammates box but would not have the gloves on. It was eating Leonard up not to be able to box but again he was putting his trust in the wisdom of CB.

In order to become a top flight professional type boxer; Leonard needed to grow emotionally, mentally, spiritually, and physically. Physical growth was inevitable but the other areas needed to be developed. Since being in PSP, CB had become an avid reader. After training one day Conrad pulled Leonard to the side.

"Leonard, what's the last book you've read?" CB asked.

"Not sure? Probably a book back in elementary school." Leonard hesitantly admitted.

"Along with physical training, you need mental training. You already know that in order to be an effective boxer you need discipline. Not only does discipline need to be developed but it has to be sustained." CB asserted.

"CB, what is it that you want me to do?" Leonard asked.

"I need you to read. The first book I want you to read is the autobiography of Malcolm X. It was written by Alex Haley."

"Oh yeah he's the cat that wrote Roots." Leonard reluctantly exclaimed.

"Exactly! This book will help cultivate the discipline you'll need to be a good boxer at PSP and maybe beyond." CB confirmed.

"I'll start tonight right after dinner." Leonard said with excitement.

"I'll drop the book off to you after dinner. Understand that this is the 1st step to creating the new you. Fuck that street shit right now Leonard. We have 11 weeks until your first fight and we need to get you right. Keep working and leave the bullshit alone. After you finish reading the book we are going to look into getting your high school diploma. You'll be getting out one day and a diploma is necessary on the street. I'll see you after dinner."

Leonard was a little apprehensive about reading the book because his reading level wasn't that high. He never cared for school. He was a master of street smarts but was lacking in book knowledge. The last thing he thought about during prison intake was getting a high school diploma. All he wanted to do was survive and maybe make it to parole in 5 years. Now he was sitting in his cell thinking about books and school; 2 things he had no desire for. But he was willing to do what CB said. CB was now a father figure for Leonard and Leonard wanted to do whatever it took to hit the heavy bag. Leonard wasn't at the level where he fully understood everything that CB was saying but he knew that CB had his best interest at heart. For the first time in 17 years Leonard felt like he had some confidence. Like most young criminals, Leonard lacked self-confidence and self-esteem. He bullied other people because his home life was fucked up and he was angry. Many nights he would sit in his cell knowing that at times, it was better than being back in the projects. Now that he was an official member of the PSP boxing team and had a single cell, he had a feeling of safety and he could sleep through the night. He knew he could kick his cellmate's ass (if he had one); he was always on point due to his experiences in juvenile detention and lessons the old heads told him before he got sent to PSP.

CB brought him the book. Leonard let CB know that he wasn't the best reader. CB told him it was cool and if there was anything he didn't understand he would explain. CB stayed and dropped science for a few minutes. Lights out was at 9:00 pm so Leonard had two hours to get some reading in. CB told Leonard that he would get him a lamp so he could read after hours. CB encouraged Leonard to take notes on the book and read things twice if needed. Leonard was scared but excited. He never paid attention to black leaders, politics, or religion. As he would soon find out, this book would touch on all three.

Chapter 3
Discipline,

"Anytime you find someone more successful than you are, especially when you're both engaged in the same business - you know they're doing something that you aren't."

"It is only after slavery and prison that the sweetest appreciation of freedom can come."

"So early in my life, I had learned that if you want something, you had better make some noise."

These were all quotes from the autobiography of Malcolm X. Leonard read the book in a little over 4 days. He was prepared to read the book again and maybe a third time. He wrote down the above quotes in his notebook and wanted to live his life the way Malcolm X did. He was intrigued that Malcolm X was in prison but got out and changed his life. It was 1988 and up until this point, Leonard never thought much about his future and reforming himself. He knew that eventually he would be in state prison so therefore there was no need to change when he got out of juvenile lockup. Reading about Malcolm X's life helped Leonard gain perspective on how a black man's life should be lived. He was 6 weeks away from being 18 and he knew that to avoid life in PSP, he had to make lifestyle changes.

Self-discipline was now necessary for Leonard to excel in and out of PSP. He knew he wasn't eligible for parole until 1993 so he had five years before he could think of life on the outside. After he finished the last page of the book, Leonard told himself out loud that he would model his life after Malcolm X and would also be a Muslim and never eat pork again.

"CB, thanks for suggesting that book. I learned a lot about Malcolm X. I wrote down some quotes from the book. If you don't mind I'd like to read it again." Leonard happily asked.

"Leonard I'm glad you enjoyed it. Mind expansion is what all young black brothers need. The streets will have you thinking and talking about bullshit. PSP is no place to get your mind right but you have a chance. Just like Malcolm X, it's going to take discipline. What separates average boxers from the great ones is discipline. I just read an article on the basketball player Magic Johnson and he said he focuses all of his time on playing basketball. That's why he already won four championships and is working on a fifth."

"Magic is my favorite player!" Leonard exclaimed.

"Yeah the Lakers are strong but the point is Magic, Kareem, and Worthy all are focused and disciplined," CB replied. "Just like Hearns, Aaron Pryor, and Mike Tyson, in boxing; to be great, you need intensity and consistent discipline. I had it but I fucked up. You have to develop it and maintain it just like Malcolm did. You are still young and can have it inside of you to flourish."

Leonard had never been around someone as profound as CB. Leonard needed someone to give it to him straight and that's what CB did. Leonard knew that he needed to listen to CB in order to survive at PSP and beyond. CB was molding Leonard into a man and boxing was the vehicle that CB used to change Leonard's paradigm on life. Leonard was a viscous street teenager that needed discipline. Right now CB and the PSP boxing team was the only outlet for Leonard to gain discipline.

Leonard was gaining insight on how life worked and used boxing as a tool to help him change his life. Life is full of pivotal moments and meeting CB 3 weeks ago was the best thing that happened to Leonard. The weight loss for Leonard was now a way of life. His purpose at PSP was to win the California Prison Welterweight Championship and live a life full of discipline. Reading that book was a catalyst to Leonard's impending greatness; because prior to PSP, he was on a path to destruction. PSP was one of the worst prisons in the country. Upon his sentencing; Leonard had no idea if he would be alive when parole time came around. By a stroke of luck, Leonard transformed from a scared young teenager to a young man looking to better himself and now was the perfect time to do it and PSP was the place. Turning 18 next month had Leonard thinking about what it meant to be a man. The words of Malcolm X had redefined what Leonard's definition of manhood was. He was now ready to train hard and read more than ever. At that moment he finished reading the book, he knew what he wanted to be and all he could focus on was representing the PSP boxing team and making CB proud.

Chapter 4
Welterweight,

After two weeks of cardio and no glove training it was time to weigh in. The goal was 150 in order to hit the heavy bag. Leonard had fasted a couple of days and was eating a lot of fruits and vegetables so he was confident that he would make weight and be able to hit the heavy bag. At 6:15 am in the dungeon, CB and Leonard were there with the old but accurate scale. Leonard took off everything but state issued white briefs. He wasn't nervous because he had been putting the work in. CB had his glasses on and his trademark toothpick in his mouth. Leonard stepped on and CB began adjusting the scale. The slider on the scale was balancing between 151 and 150. It finally settled on 150 and both Leonard and CB were ecstatic! This meant that Leonard could now hit the heavy bag. To CB it meant that Leonard showed that he could discipline himself. The discipline also meant that Leonard would be able to dig deep in tough situations.

7:00 am and the gloves were on. Leonard was so excited CB had him take deep breaths in order to calm down. This was the first time in 7 years since Leonard put on a pair of gloves and entered a boxing ring. Leonard felt the feel of the gloves on his hands. The tape and the gauze pads fit very snug. His hands were sweating and he had to get used to the feel. It felt a little awkward for him to throw punches with these 10ounce gloves on. Back in East Oakland, on 75th & Olive, Leonard was used to slap boxing with friends and sometimes against some dudes he didn't know for money. Now being in the boxing ring he felt like he had to learn something new for the first time in life.

"Put your left foot forward, balance yourself, and snap your wrist like this. Throwing a jab isn't like a knockout punch. A jab is designed to keep your opponent from rushing in and mauling you. A jab scores points with the judges and also creates doubt in your opponent's head. Larry Holmes snapped his jab like a towel at the pool. He won on points and kept himself from getting hit all behind the jab. The jab is the tool that wins fights and keeps distance for a great boxer. Ali in his prime was the master of the jab. Ali had a punishing jab that helped create his legend. Leonard you can win the California Prison Boxing Association (CPBA) Welterweight Title by mastering the art of throwing the jab. Jabs win fights. The guy that throws and lands the most jabs typically wins the fight. Right here is where the work starts. 9 weeks until your first fight. We'll win that fight if we work hard on throwing the jab."

2 hours of actual boxing in the ring and Leonard was exhausted. It had been a long time since Leonard was that tired. He ran almost 2 miles running from the cops back in '85 and when they caught him he basically collapsed in the back of the squad car. He felt the same way now as the team prepared to go to lunch.

"CB, I'm tired. Moving around the ring is much tougher than running 2 miles around the yard."

The movement is constant and requires a change of direction." CB replied. "The legs have to be developed in order to fight 15 rounds. You saw how tired Ali was in the Thrilla of Manilla. Frazier was on his ass the whole fight and Ali kept moving each round. You're tired now without an opponent. 9 weeks to get right. You'll sleep great tonight. After lunch we'll come back to the dungeon and talk as a team. Duran and Hearns fought back in November '83. It was a tough fifteen round fight. Duran is tough son of a bitch. He made his bones as a lightweight and was now challenging the welterweight champ of the world. Duran is a warrior with the heart of a lion. He'll walk through fire in order to win a fight. That shit with Sugar Ray was something else. Not sure what happened that night but I still respect Duran. I want you guys to embody the spirit of guys like Hearns, Duran, and Frazier."

"Leonard, Thomas Hearns was on the cover of a few Ring Magazines. I'm going to let you read them because you are fighting at welterweight. Hopefully you'll pattern your game after Thomas Hearns since you 2 are built just alike."

"I can't wait to see it." Leonard replied.

The team was working out on the heavy bag and Leonard watched. CB didn't want Leonard to work out in the afternoon. CB wanted him to build up his boxing stamina. Intense morning workouts for the next 5 weeks and then a month from the fight, they'll ramp up the workouts. CB knew that Leonard would be fine mentally but he wanted to make sure that he could physically and emotionally sustain a 6 round fight. CPBA prison fights were 6 or 8 rounds and championship fights were 10-12 rounds depending on the weight. Leonard had to develop the boxing legs to last 6 rounds. There was no guarantee that he would be fighting an inexperienced fighter so CB wasn't taking any chances. Since Leonard hadn't sparred yet, CB didn't know if he could take punch. CB figured he could because he was a tough nose motherfucker from East Oakland, but still you never know how it is until you get hit. Shit changes without headgear and bigger gloves. CA prison fights were just like professional fights. No headgear and 8oz gloves. Each prison that had a boxing team took it very seriously and each team had at least 2 guys that fought in the Golden Gloves. This made the competition very intense and no trainer could afford not to have his boxers 100% prepared.

CB always felt that boxing was more mental than physical. He poured all of his knowledge into Leonard and tried to give him the psychological advantage that it took to be an extraordinary boxer. Leonard was soaking it up and was eager to learn more. Prior to meeting CB, Leonard wasn't a student of boxing and only knew about Sugar Ray Leonard and Muhammad Ali because they were all over television. When he was 11 years old his trainer told Leonard that he had talent and could be good one day. By the age of 13, Leonard was in the streets and lost the desire to keep up with boxing. Leonard took that Ring Magazine CB gave him back to his cell and started reading the article on Thomas Hearns. The article went in depth regarding Hearns's upbringing and his entire professional career. Leonard was excited to learn that Hearns came from a tough upbringing much like himself. Hearns had an unparalleled work ethic and that is how Leonard wanted to be. Hearns turned pro at the age of 19 and never looked back.

As Leonard sat on the edge of his cot reading every word of the article he began to envision what it would be like to be a professional boxer. The Hearns article made Leonard create a vision of excellence in his head. Hearns was the #1 welterweight in the world for many years and now Leonard wanted to be the #1 welterweight in the CA prison system. The excitement led Leonard to do push-ups through the rest of the night. Each time he pushed himself up he let his mind wander to being the best welterweight in the California prison system. He was hoping CB would let him keep that Ring Magazine so he could put a picture of Hearns in his cell. Hearns was now who Leonard wanted to be like. Leonard was now solely focused on being a welterweight champion for PSP and then maybe, just maybe, welterweight champ of the world like Hearns!

<h1 style="text-align:center">Chapter 5</h1>

Letters,

Training was going very well. Leonard was beginning to incorporate more meat into his diet because he was right around the 150-weight limit to fight at welterweight. 5 weeks until his first fight and one more week until he would be training twice a day. The heavy bag and pad work were part of his daily routine and in a few days CB would know the name of his opponent and some background information. Information on the opponent would help CB better prepare Leonard for the fight. Upon returning to his cell, Leonard saw an envelope on his floor. In his 5 months at PSP Leonard had one visit from one of his two sisters and one letter from a girl he was dating back home. Once training started Leonard wasn't worried about his girl or his family. He never had a great relationship with his parents because of their alcohol and drug abuse.

He gave a head nod to his Hearns picture on his wall and sat on his cot and opened the letter. It was from his oldest sister Yvonne. Yvonne was 21 and was attending Laney College in Oakland. Somehow Yvonne was able to stay on the straight and narrow and keep her head above water. Yvonne always supported Leonard and was there each time he went to court. Leonard had a special bond with Yvonne and was proud of her being in college. They both knew that it was almost impossible to make it out of the Haney Projects in East Oakland. The Haney projects were notorious throughout the city for breeding straight killers. The fact that Leonard and his two sisters were alive was minor miracle. Leonard cleared his mind and unfolded the letter.

"Hey Leonard. How are you making out? I've been praying for you every day. Alicia and Marvin said that you haven't called

home in a few weeks. I haven't been home in a couple of weeks. I've been staying on campus. I left right after the New Year. I drove down to Los Angeles with a friend I met at Laney. Her name is Claudette and she's real cool. I told her about our situation back home and she said it was cool to stay the week up there until was time for us to back to Laney. I told her all about you and she started praying for you too. Her 1st cousin is locked up at Polley Island. It's not like PSP. Polley is like a county jail. People only stay there for a year or two. He's 20 and looking at a life sentence for murder. I'm glad that you can get out in 5 years. Even though I was praying, I knew that you would be OK. You're a survivor Leonard and I know you'll find a way to make it out in 5 years.

I graduate next June and I've been thinking about moving down south. I talked to Aunt Janette and she said I could move with her and Uncle John down in Atlanta. I've been working part-time at a restaurant on International BLVD. I've been saving money and I'm going to buy a car next year. The niggas on the bus be stinking and the BART people are creepy at night. I'll be driving the car I buy down to Atlanta. After I get down there I'm going to apply to go to nursing school. When you get out you could move down there with me. Cousin Scooter has a cleaning business in the Atlanta area and he said he would hook you up. I know you aren't thinking about that right now, I just wanted to let you know that I'm here to help.

I hope you haven't been talking to that bitch that claims to be your girlfriend. She's been out here messing with a bunch of dudes. I saw her on Piedmont Ave and she said she missed you and wanted to come to PSP and visit. I told her that she would have to check with you. You can do what you want but I would leave her alone. She's no good for you and you don't need that stress. Are you going to get your HS diploma? You're going to need that. Times are changing and jobs are making sure that you have a diploma before they hire you. If you want I'll help you study for the GED test. It's a test that equals all that you've learned in High School. Passing the test is just like getting your diploma. It's something you should really look into.

I'm so excited that next week you'll be 18! I had my doubts that you would make it; especially after you got stabbed last year.

We were all so scared but you pulled through like you always do. Shit is changing out here Leonard. These dudes aren't fighting like they used to. More guns are being pulled and dudes are even shooting at the police. Who knows how it will be when you get out in '93? There is a new radio station called Power 103 and they play all of the new young people stuff. They were playing "My Philosophy" by Boogie Down Productions and "Straight Outta Compton" by NWA. I like it because they play all the stuff we can dance to and not that old Motown stuff that Mommy & Daddy played around the house.

Well I'll talk to you later and remember I love you! HAPPY BIRTHDAY LITTLE BROTHER!!!"
-Love Yvonne

Leonard choked up after reading the letter from his sister. He loves his family but has blocked out the negative thoughts of his home-life. Right now all he could focus on was being the CA prison welterweight champ. However he loves both of his sisters so he decided that he would write Yvonne back.

"Hey Vonne. Good to hear from you. Miss you and glad you're cool. Moving to Atlanta sounds like a plan. Started boxing again and it keeps me busy. I met this cat CB from LA and he's a boxing trainer. He been schooling me since I been here. Wish he was my pop. He dropped a couple books on me and they hella good. He been here since he was 18 so he knows how to deal with these cats. He wanna keep me on the straight and narrow. I'm seriously thinking about turning to Islam.

If it wasn't for boxing this stretch would be hella-hella tough. This place is rough. Some dude got shanked to death the other day out in the yard. They don't fuck with the boxing team but the gangs up here don't fuck around. Shit can get crazy in a minute. I have my first fight February 14th. I'm hella nervous but looking forward to it. I'm ready to whoop some ass!

Fuck that bitch Shante. She been a trick and I used to hit that drunk. I wrote her my first two weeks up here but stopped when I joined the boxing team. She can go fly a kite for all I care. Imma tryta get my GED up here. They have classes that start in

April. That should be a good look for parole in '93. I'm going to keep all of the letters that you write to show the parole board. I'll write to you before my fight. How was the funeral? How's Marvin?
-Love Leonard

Chapter 6
Preparation,

Leonard's first fight was only ten days away. CB let him know that training would be winding down. Leonard was weighing 158. CB wanted him to be exactly 150 on the day of the weigh-in, which was Friday, February 19, 1988. Each member of the team had multiple fights. The CA Prison System was proud of the success of the boxing tournaments and fights were typically scheduled every 10 weeks except for during the holiday season. The PSP team under CB's leadership had only lost 5 fights since the inception of the team. CB was a master at making adjustments during the fight. He had a keen sense of how to gauge the tactics of the opposition and effectively communicate with his fighters. CB was also a master motivator and strategist. For the other inmates it was a time to socialize and bullshit, but for CB it was work and his life's passion. He mimicked himself after Eddie Futch (Joe Frazier's trainer) and specifically, Angelo Dundee (Sugar Ray Leonard's trainer). Back in '81 when Leonard was fighting Hearns, after the 12th round when Leonard came back to the corner, Dundee told Leonard; "We got 9 minutes, you're blowing it son, you're blowing it." After that round Leonard punished Hearns for the next 5 minutes and stopped him in the 14th.

CB cared about his fighters and wanted them to be prepared. He knew all about boxers dying in the ring and that was the last thing he wanted for anyone on his team. That's why defense and stamina were preached so heavily. CB believed that in order to maintain the proper defense throughout a fight, you needed stamina to keep your energy up. Teaching someone offensive technique was easy. Most men that took up boxing as a sport were born with the ability to throw a punch. What separated the special boxers like Ali and Leonard from the rest was their ability to duck a punch. CB remembered Ali's younger days when he was super slick and barely took punishment. In his later years, he engaged more but in his prime he was a defensive wizard. CB made defense the motto and mantra of the PSP team. That's why it took weeks before Leonard could hit the heavy bag. The heavy bag, although part of the daily routine, wasn't the major training component for CB. For CB it was all about the mental preparation.

"Leonard, boxing is unlike any other sport. In football and basketball if you're losing you can call a timeout. In boxing there aren't any timeouts. Three minutes per round and then a one-minute break. The bell rings and it's back out there - life or death. Many times throughout the course of a fight a boxer will question his purpose in the ring. He questions if he can take another punch. He questions if he can throw another punch. He questions his existence. If the fight goes the distance it's the longest 36 - 45 minutes of his life. In the prison system however, you have 12 minutes to dig deep and get the win. This is the 12 minutes where you prove to yourself as a boxer that you made the right choices and validate all of our training and preparation. All the hard work we put in will manifest itself in the ring. In 10 days it's show time! I want to you start preparing yourself for the mental aspect of the sport. Over the next 9 days we'll slow down on the physical training and strictly prepare to go to war for 18 minutes. But remember while they are playing checkers we'll be playing chess. We'll be one step ahead. We'll be thinking about the punches before they come. Defense and stamina Leonard; defense and stamina are how we win. We stay clean and we outwork our opponent."

CB spent the entire afternoon pouring all of his philosophy into Leonard. CB wanted to make sure that Leonard understood everything he needed to before he got into the ring. The ring could be a brutal and unforgiving place. The ring was nowhere for a man to be if he didn't have the intestinal fortitude to go the distance. CB was planting seeds in Leonard. He wanted to make sure that Leonard was prepared mentally as well as physically. Leonard hadn't been in a ring in 7 years. That layoff was concerning to CB but he had full faith in Leonard and could tell Leonard had full confidence in himself.

After dinner Leonard did his normal routine by going back to his cell and reading. Leonard was reading "The Art of War" by Sun Tzu. CB gave to this Leonard in order to get his head right for the fight. Leonard began writing down quotes just like he did when reading the Malcolm X book. " No long war ever profited any country: 100 victories in 100 battles are simply ridiculous. Anyone who excels in defeating his enemies triumphs before his enemy's threats becomes real". Leonard wanted to implement this tactical strategy into his first fight. 8 more nights of sleep and that 9th morning Leonard would wake up and it would be the day of the fight. CB told Leonard about meditating and deep breathing. This was to help Leonard concentrate solely on his opponent. Sun Tzu also discussed the power of focusing on your opponent in his book. Leonard was solely thinking about Grady Sampson his opponent on February 19th.

Grady was 23 years old and was doing a 12-year sentence for burglary and aggravated assault. Grady had fought three previous times and had a record of 2-1. CB had scouted him so Leonard knew what to prepare for. Grady was an all-out brawler that liked to come forward. CB compared him to a mix between Aaron Pryor and Joe Frazier. Both men were short in stature but had unbelievable heart. However, Grady wasn't as skilled as either one of those champion fighters. Grady liked to keep pressure on his opponents but that was tailor made for Leonard's style.

Defense and stamina were the words written on the walls of the dungeon. Leonard was locked into what he needed to do. Grady Sampson was now his daily obsession and the combination of CB and Sun Tzu had Leonard thinking like a deadly boxing sniper. Leonard planned on winning his first bout. He made sure focused on being patient and listening to CB. Leonard was scared and nervous; similar to the way he felt when he entered PSP. And just like that day, he was scared more of the unknown. He was scared that he might not execute the way CB wanted him to. He was nervous about fighting in front of a crowd. He had confidence in his ability but he was still a teenager and learning about how to function as a boxer. In the ring there were very specific rules about what you can and can't do. On the street Leonard didn't give a fuck. He would fight with his hands or whatever was available. One time he hit a dude over the head with an empty bottle. Another time he slashed a dude with a pocketknife after school. But now it would just him and Grady. CB told him to embrace that fear and nervous energy and use it to his advantage. Fear helps men fight better. "If you feel like they are going to take something from you it's easy to rumble in the ring" said CB. Leonard was replaying all of CB's wisdom in his ear. 9 days and it was time to execute Grady Sampson!

<h1 style="text-align:center">Chapter 7</h1>

First Fight,

It was time for those 3 months of training and mental preparation to pay off. The day was here. It was time to see if Leonard was ready to fulfill the potential that CB thought he had. It was time for Leonard to see what he was made of. Did the hard work in the dungeon prepare a boxing champ? Training was over. The reading was over. In a few hours it was time for Leonard and Grady to show off.

The fights were at the Fulton State Penitentiary outside of San Jose, Ca. Fulton State was an old school prison that was built on a farm. The gym was in a transformed barn-house. The lighting and ventilation were both poor. There were quite a few fight posters on the wall. The warden (John Brady) at Fulton State was a huge boxing fan and was high school friends with boxing promoter Bob Arum. Arum donated fight posters from some of the biggest fights of the 70's and 80's. Leonard/Duran, Leonard/Hearns, Ali/Spinks, Hearns/Antuofermo, Pryor/Arguello, Holmes/Shavers & Holmes/ Cooney were all on the wall. Brady wanted the barn-house to remain dingy because it reminded him of the fight houses from the 30's & 40's.

PSP took a prison bus down there early on February 19, 1988. They weren't handcuffed but there were two prison guards with shotguns at both ends of the bus. Typically, members of the boxing team weren't flight risks due to the possibility of parole, but guards were still present during all boxing team transportation. The guards were also armed and present during the boxing matches. Each prison supplied two guards per team. Fight time was set for 1:30 pm. All the fights that day were four round fights so every half hour a new fight would begin. There was no locker room like the professionals had; each prison team was together in the back of the gym. The barn-house still had original wood floors that would creak when the boxers jumped rope and jogged in place.

Former Heavyweight Contender Gerry Cooney would be at Fulton State today. He enjoyed the prison fights in New York, New Jersey, and Pennsylvania. He also loved flying to the West Coast and watching the California fighters. He was treated like royalty and many of the prison boxers got his autograph. He knew CB from attending the fights since the late 70's. He saw CB working with the team in the back of the barn-house and approached.

"CB, how ya doin man?" Cooney asked.

"I'm doing good Gerry. That Holmes fight was tough. That son of a bitch can fight! Gerry you can come back. I have faith in you."

"Thanks CB. I really appreciate the kind words. I tried hard against Larry. His jab was better than I thought. I hit him with my best shot and he took it. I would've beaten any other heavyweight that night. I'm looking to come back later this year. Who's the new guy?"

"This is Leonard, and he's our new welterweight. He's a beast and a good listener. He just turned 18 and he has a great right hand."

"Leonard, it's nice to meet you." Gerry said with a smile.

"Hello Mr. Cooney it's a pleasure to meet you." Leonard excitedly replied.

"Call me Gerry. CB is a great man. Make sure you listen to him and defend yourself at all times in the ring."

"Thanks Gerry. I will."

"I will Talk to you later CB. Leonard, I look forward to seeing your fight. Good luck."

Leonard was nervous but focused. He would be up in two more fights. There was already a knockout in the 1st round. The prisoners loved the action and the violence but the PSP team was known for being technicians in the ring. Defense and stamina were the principles for the team. Leonard was soaking it all in. 7 months ago he was on the streets of East Oakland stealing from and assaulting people. It was surreal for him to be in this position. He knew he would wind up in prison but he never imagined PSP would re-ignite his love for boxing. The ring was now the only place where Leonard would assault anyone. He promised CB that he wouldn't get into any shit at PSP. He wanted to keep his promise to CB because he knew that he would kick him off of the team. Leonard wanted to do everything he could to make CB proud of him. Today was the day to take a huge step in changing his life around.

The atmosphere resembled the old Roman Coliseum. The crowd wanted blood and they cheered for it at every moment. Most of the prisoners weren't fans of boxing; they just thrived on the violence that boxing offered. The knockout earlier in the day sent them in frenzy and satisfied their bloodthirsty nature. Fortunately for CA prison boxing, so far there were no incidents at the fights. Only a model prisoner was permitted to attend the fights. The gangs were deep in California. They had to be careful on who attended fights. Most of the guys going to the fights would one day be up for parole so most likely they would be on their best behavior. Dwight Braxton was a Prison champ in New Jersey in the late 70's and went onto win the light-heavyweight championship. The prisoners knew this and made sure they paid attention to every fighter. If one of them went onto success as a pro, they could talk shit on the streets and tell their boys they saw that dude in the prison fights. This was prison so gambling on the fights was plenty prevalent and even threats to certain fighters. The crowd was excited and ready for more action after the knockout.

"Time for wraps Leonard" CB said as he rubbed his goatee and maintained laser focus in his eyes. CB noticed Grady at the other end of the gym. He looked like he weighed at least 170. Leonard was a trim and fit 150. CB knew that their motto would be huge during this fight. Based on the size of Grady, Leonard would have to stick and move. Because Grady was a come forward fighter, Leonard's defense was going to be very necessary. CB would soon be giving Leonard his last words of advice before the bell rang.

Leonard had his hands on the table as CB started to wrap them.

"Leonard, think about where you were this time last year. Think about all that we've done in the gym. Think about all the books you've read. Now is the 1st step to you changing your life. You can be whomever you want in life but in that ring today you need to be the best defensive fighter in the world. Grady is bigger, older, and stronger than you but he doesn't have your skill. Rely on your talent. Maintain your discipline and have faith in your training. You are ready for this. After your hands are wrapped we are going to hit the pads and work up a sweat."

"CB, I won't let you down. Grady is losing today!"

Leonard worked up a sweat on the pads and the whole time him and CB chanted defense & stamina. The PSP team was there to support Leonard. They knew he had talent and that he was the man even though he was only 18. Leonard had potential and today was the day to begin to realize that potential. Leonard was sweating and had a strong look of determination in his eyes. CB knew that Leonard was ready. The last fight was in the last round and in seven minutes it would be time. CB took off the pads and grabbed his stool and spit bucket. Leonard's gloves were on and he was pacing in the back. The decision was read on the 1:00 pm fight and the ref signaled for CB & Leonard. CB grabbed Leonard's head and pulled his ear close to his mouth, "Defense and stamina." They walked to the ring and in a few minutes Leonard would be facing Grady.

Chapter 8
Jab,

This wasn't like professional prize fighting with an entourage and music. There was no singing of the national anthem. There were no fancy trunks or boots. Leonard and CB and Grady and his trainer were the only ones in the ring along with the referee. The referee was a professional who was paid by the day. The California State Athletic Commission worked in conjunction with the California Prison Boxing Association to make sure everything was done right. There was also a professional ring announcer to give it the feel of a true boxing match. The crowd was ready for the next fight. As with every fight they were hoping for a knockout.

Leonard had a steely focus much like Thomas Hearns when he fought. Leonard was taking this very serious and he seemed wise beyond his years. Grady was staring at Leonard trying to intimidate him. They locked eyes and displayed the type of stare down you would see in a high profile match. Fulton State was the testing ground to determine how much Leonard had learned and how good he could be.

"Fighting out of the red corner representing Patton State Penitentiary, from Oakland, California… Leonard Smith."

"Fighting out of the blue corner representing Fulton State Penitentiary, from Richmond, California with a record of 2-1… Grady Sampson."

After the announcements both fighters and their trainers met with the referee in the center of the ring. The referee told them that he wanted them to keep it clean and protect themselves at all times. He also told them to obey his command at all times. He told them to touch gloves and go back to their respective corners.

Grady had a look of death in his eyes and was intent on intimidating Leonard. At the middle of the ring Grady said "I'm going to fuck you up young boy!" Leonard didn't respond. CB had told him not to engage in any shit talking prior to the bout. The goal was to talk with the fists inside the ring. "Beat Grady and you can talk shit after the fight!"

CB placed the mouthpiece in Leonard's mouth. Leonard was scared, nervous, sweating but ready. Leonard didn't fear any man, he only feared letting CB down.

"Leonard, This mother fucker is going to come straight at you. Jab him, step to the left and land that right hand. He likes to overwhelm people. Defense and stamina is going to win us this fight."

Leonard gave CB a head nod and a wink. CB slapped his gloves, the bell rang and the fight was on. Grady came storming out of his corner just like CB said he would. He threw a couple of wild shots at Leonard and Leonard made him miss his first two punches.

"Stay off the ropes" yelled CB. Leonard pivoted to his left and threw his first jab. The jab snapped Grady's head back and made him reset his feet. Leonard threw two more jabs and each jab snapped Grady's head back. The crowd got excited when Leonard landed those three jabs. "Keep jabbing" CB yelled. Grady was still coming forward and looked even more frustrated that he couldn't land a shot on Leonard. Grady threw a body shot that caught Leonard right around the midsection. Leonard took a deep breath and slid to his left. Grady threw another punch that missed and he stumbled a bit. Leonard hit him with another jab. Grady pushed Leonard to the ropes and threw a bunch of punches that landed around Leonard's shoulder but none to his face. Leonard tied Grady up by grabbing his arms and that forced the referee to break them up. There was 1 minute and 45 seconds left in the 1st round. Grady was breathing hard but relentless. Leonard was calm and focused on the goal. He had thoughts of Hearns in Ring Magazine with the belts around his waist and visualized this as he tied Grady up. In his mind he knew Grady wasn't going to beat him. Leonard just had to stick to the plan that CB put in place.

Leonard was off the ropes and back to moving and giving Grady angles so it would be difficult for him to be hit. Leonard continued to pump the left jab. He hadn't thrown the right hand yet. Still only pumping the left jab. Anyone watching could see that Leonard was clearly winning the fight but Grady was always dangerous and it was only the first round. Leonard was on the ropes again and once more decided to tie up, which frustrated Grady. As the referee broke them up, Grady threw a punch that caught Leonard right on his chin. Leonard wasn't dazed by it but CB yelled for the ref to take a point. The ref gave Grady a warning and it was back to action. After getting hit, Leonard shook his head and smacked his gloves together. His only intent was to win the fight regardless of what tactics Grady used. CB told Leonard that dirty tactics would be a possibility and to remain calm no matter what Grady tried. With 30 seconds left in the round Leonard threw his first right hand that rocked Grady! CB was excited and told Leonard to follow up. Leonard threw a left right combination that sent Grady reeling. Leonard was patient and now he was the aggressor. Grady threw a wild left haymaker that Leonard ducked. Leonard followed with a stiff jab. Leonard was now looking for the knockout! Grady had the heart of a Lion and kept coming forward. As Leonard was setting up for another right hand the bell rang.

Leonard went back to the corner and CB was overly excited. "Leonard that was fantastic. You remained calm and stuck to the plan. He's going to come out more determined this round. It's your job to discourage him. Use his aggression against him. Stay off of the ropes and stay with the jab. There will be an opening for a right hand you'll see it and when you do land it. The next right hand you throw will be the end of the fight. Don't lose focus!" Leonard shook his head in acknowledgement. CB put his mouthpiece back in and it was time for round two.

The bell rang for round two and it started much like round one. Grady came out like a man possessed and threw 15 straight punches without Leonard throwing back. None of them landed clean but it looked good for the crowd. Leonard used his forearms and pushed Grady off of him and landed a quick left jab. This time Grady walked through it and landed a sharp right to Leonard's chest. Leonard was stunned and took a few steps back. As Grady rushed in Leonard once again tied him up. The referee stepped in and broke them up. Leonard landed a quick right-left combination that momentarily stopped Grady in his tracks. Grady kept pushing forward and threw another wild left haymaker. Leonard sidestepped the haymaker and threw a right jab. Leonard then threw a left to the body that caught Grady right near his liver. The punch paralyzed Grady and there was the opportunity that CB talked about. Leonard could see the opening for the right hand.

Leonard threw the right hand but it seemed like it was in slow motion. He summoned all the strength he had in his body. He envisioned Grady entering his cell to rape him or kill him and that fueled his aggression. Leonard had anger in his fists and malice in his heart as the punch was in the air. Everyone could see it coming and Grady couldn't get out of the way. The punch landed and all the prisoners jumped to their feet in adulation. The sound was deafening. The referee began counting and simultaneously directed Leonard to go to the neutral corner. Leonard was poised as he waited to see if Grady would get up. "…6, 7, 8, 9, you're out!" The ref shouted. Leonard had done it. His first prison fight had ended in a knockout. In his wildest dreams he couldn't have imagined that he would be part of a boxing team and win his first bout by KO. CB preached defense and stamina and didn't require his boxers automatically go for a knockout. CB had a systematic approach to wearing the opponent down throughout the bout. CB always prepared for a fight to go the distance but this was extra special for CB. He was proud of Leonard's discipline and the hard work that he put in.

After the ref finished counting CB jumped in the ring and picked Leonard up and carried him around the ring. The prisoners were still clapping and the doctor at Fulton State was checking out Grady. Leonard went back to his corner and sat on his stool. CB took his mouthpiece out but left his gloves on. Leonard wanted to keep his gloves on. Knocking Grady out was a different feeling for Leonard. He had knocked out plenty of people on the street but they were easy targets. Grady was a dangerous dude and he was there to hurt Leonard. Leonard felt that sense of accomplishment sitting on the stool but did a great job of keeping his composure and maintaining his emotions. CB was very obviously elated and he didn't know what to do with himself. He looked like Jim Valvano after NC State won the NCAA championship in 1983. He was so excited he ran around the court looking for someone to hug. That's how CB looked but the ring only had a few people in it. The rest of the boxing team was in the back celebrating but weren't allowed in the ring. This was prison and not Las Vegas, but it didn't matter to CB and Leonard they knew they accomplished what they came to do -win.

In the back of the room the PSP boxing team all congratulated Leonard. The entire team fought that day. Leonard was the only one to score a knockout. CB felt like a proud papa that his whole team won. He had a special place for Leonard because he was the youngest. CB knew that he had the most potential and was the hardest worker on the team. Gerry Cooney came to the back to congratulate CB & Leonard.

"Awesome right hand, Leonard. What's in there; dynamite?" Gerry chuckled as he congratulated Leonard.

"Thanks Gerry, I just threw it the way CB taught me." Leonard said proudly.

"When I see Hearns I'm going to tell him he better retire before you get out." Gerry said.

"Hearns is the guy I look up to. I have pictures of him on my wall in my cell." Leonard said with pride.

"He is an awesome champion and someone you should pattern your boxing career after.

Hearns is no joke and he worked hard for everything that he has. Keep working hard and listening to CB." Gerry said with a huge smile.

"I plan on it Gerry."

"CB and Leonard, I'll see you both next month in Hazeltown."

CB said "Hey Gerry you tell Larry you want a rematch. "Gerry laughed and went back to ringside. Leonard was quiet and thought about how fast his heart was beating. He knew that the adrenaline was pumping fast. He couldn't wait until his next fight. It was a euphoric state in the area where the PSP team was assembled. Even the armed guards that rode up on the bus with the team congratulated Leonard. It had been quite a while since CB was this giddy regarding a new fighter. CB was desperate to have a California Prison Boxing Association Champion on his team. To have a CPBA champion would make all of the years CB had left that much easier. CB told the team that they could all eat snack foods for the next few days. They wouldn't be doing any sparring for a week. Training would still be part of the daily routine but that wouldn't commence until Tuesday morning. This day was all about celebration. Leonard's victory was the culmination of 3 months of intensity and focus.

CB took Leonard's gloves off and had him soak his hands in ice. Leonard sat in the corner by himself and reflected on the fight. Grady was a tough son of a bitch and had some pop in his punches. Leonard knew that he did well but had a long way to go before he could be like his idol Thomas Hearns. At 18, Leonard finally had some purpose in his life. He knew, at minimum, he would be boxing for PSP for the next 4.5 years. Reflection time was over and the goodwill that had been established at Fulton would be left there. It was time to go back to PSP. Leonard knew that danger was always eminent at PSP. He didn't have to worry about getting in fights but the possibility for getting shanked was always there. The reality for Leonard was that he was still prisoner #641938 and his cell was on the second floor of the housing unit at PSP, but all Leonard was focused on was being CPBA Welterweight Champion by the end of 1989.

Back at PSP CB gave Leonard a hug, something that rarely happens in a prison environment. Leonard's father hadn't hugged him since he was a little boy. Leonard felt good that he made CB proud. Leonard was determined to stay focused and stay disciplined.

"Leonard I'm proud of you. Grady was a tough son of a bitch and you weathered the storm. You showed that you could handle adversity and survive. We have 6 weeks until your next fight. The next fight will be here at PSP. I'll find out whom you're fighting on Tuesday. They have to check the results from all the fights this weekend. Try and get some sleep. Don't do any physical activity until we get back to the dungeon. Again I'm proud of you son."

"Thanks for having faith in me CB. I want to win that PPBA Welterweight title for you." "I hear you son but let's take it one fight at a time. Good night Leonard."

42

Chapter 9

CPBA Champ,

Leonard sat on his cot and reflected on every aspect of the fight. He thought about Grady coming forward, his moves in the ring, his meeting Gerry Cooney and all that his winning meant to CB. Since he was still 18, like any 18 year old, Leonard wanted some snacks. It had been 3 months since Leonard had any junk food. CB said they could relax and snack for a few days since the entire team went undefeated at Fulton. Leonard enjoyed his snacks from the commissary. He loved junk food back in Oakland. He dug into a pack of Twinkies and Hostess cupcakes. He felt relieved that the fight was over. For just a few days he wanted to be a teenager. He was still basking in the glow of his first victory and was enjoying the fact that his hard work paid off. He knew that it would take a tremendous amount of effort to realize the goal of becoming CPBA Welterweight Champion.

The next few days Leonard was treated like a star at PSP. The most hardened of lifers gave Leonard a handshake and congratulated him on his first victory. Word had spread through PSP that Leonard was the real deal. His right hand, which they saw first-hand in the mess hall, was becoming legendary after only one official CPBA fight. Leonard remained humble at PSP. CB had told him many times that one fight doesn't make you a champion but one fight can ruin your career. CB reminded him to remain grounded and always stay focused no matter what the circumstances were. The attention was inspiration for Leonard to win the title.

Typically boxers take at least 8 weeks for a training camp but the CPBA boxing schedule wasn't conducive for boxers to take that much time off. They fought either monthly or bi-monthly. The CPBA officials knew that most of the fighters were younger and could handle the pace of the schedule. The prison trainers had the option to sit the boxers three times a year. A boxer had to fight at least six times a year in order to be eligible to win a CPBA title. The entire PSP team was in great shape so CB didn't have to push them super hard in the dungeon. For the next three weeks they would focus more on technique and mental discipline. CB wanted to keep their hands strong and their bodies refreshed. The competition would increase as the months moved on. There was an agreement in place for a welterweight tournament to be established in the beginning of 1989. The current champion, Tyler Mack, was being released in December of '88. Therefore the title would be vacant and thus, the need for a tournament. CB had his eye on the tournament. Leonard was the only member of the team eligible for a title shot next year. The others would have to work their way up because of their records. CB had a paper taped to the dungeon wall that read ***Vacant Welterweight Title 1/1/89 Who wants it***?

The victory tour was over at PSP and it was time for Leonard and the team to get back in the dungeon. The scene in the Dungeon was familiar. The dust still kicked up when the boxers were jumping rope. The boxing ring floor still felt like concrete and Conrad was still focused. CB welcomed everyone back with his LA type of handshake. He would shake your hand then grab it and give it a light smack with the other hand. Leonard never asked CB why he did this. Leonard thought maybe it was just something he did to reassure his guys that he had their back. Every boxer at PSP knew that CB cared about him and had his best interest at heart. CB was the reason that Leonard had survived at PSP as long as he had. The dungeon was the sanctuary for all of the boxers. They were back to the grind and it was time to gear up for the next fight in 3 weeks. After putting his shoes on and taping his hands Leonard saw the paper that CB taped to the wall. He gave CB a look and a head nod. That head nod let CB know that Leonard would be the one to get the vacant title.

Leonard maintained his same pace throughout training. He knew he could take a punch and more importantly he knew he had the ability to hurt his opponent. Training was an outlet for

Leonard. He used training as a time to put his home life out of his mind. Nights in his cell he wished that his father wasn't an alcoholic or his mom a heroin addict. He wished that he had a place to call home. He wished that he lived in San Leandro with his Aunt instead of Oakland. He wished that he had the guidance to steer him away from the streets. All of those wishes dissipated when Leonard was training. The heavy bag remained the vice for Leonard. Hitting the heavy bag equated to him punching the negativity out his mind.

When Leonard jogged through the yard the inmates yelled his name. Leonard would give them a fist pump and keep on jogging. It was weird to Leonard that PSP felt like home. The place he knew he would end up but was scared to death to enter now felt like home. Now that he was the #1 boxer at PSP, he felt there was a bond that he created with other inmates. He didn't speak to them much but there was an unspoken respect that was between them. Leonard still knew that some inmates didn't give a fuck about the boxing team. PSP wasn't a summer camp. PSP still equaled danger and Leonard knew to keep his movements measured and specific. CB constantly reminded the team what life at PSP was all about. The reality of prison life never escaped CB or the team. CB wasn't into any prison bullshit and required the same of his the members of the team. Regardless of how good the PSP team was for morale, the inmates were never to be fully trusted. Letting your guard down for a minute could get you killed. The warden loved CB so much that he set it up for each team member to have his own cell. That way at least they wouldn't have to worry about getting shanked in their sleep.

Leonard was strictly focused on the CPBA championship. The realities of prison life never escaped him but training for the championship was paramount to life or death for Leonard. Leonard needed to block everything out and focus on each individual fight and eventually on the tournament for 1989. He scribbled 1989 on his cell wall right next to his picture of Thomas Hearns. In his mind Hearns would help get him to the title. Leonard was ready. The only thing standing between him and the championship was time. In his mind time was the only impediment to the title. Although he only had one fight his mind was focused on the bigger picture. He had to slow down and remind himself to take it one fight at a time and more importantly one round at a time. He knew that CB only focused on the next fight. CB wouldn't entertain any championship talk until it was time. For Leonard the time was now!

It was December 1988 and Leonard had done what he said he was going to do. His record was 7-0 throughout the year with 5 KO's. He was right there on the cusp of fighting for the CPBA welterweight champ. Due to winning seven straight fights Leonard was eligible for fighting for the title in 1988. PSP was buzzing! Since the inception of the boxing team at PSP there hadn't been a welterweight champ. Everyone who cared at PSP recognized that Leonard was in line to be the first welterweight champ ever at PSP. CB knew that the powers that be at PSP were pulling for Leonard to put PSP on the map within the California prison boxing system. To have a champ at your prison equated to big time publicity for the warden. Local newspapers and TV stations would always cover the CPBA title tournaments. The wardens would be interviewed and maybe even their prison would be spotlighted for local and national news.

"Welcome to the office Leonard." Warden Dennis welcomed Leonard to his office that was adjacent to the prison. The office was huge and represented the images of a man that was born and raised on the west coast. There was a huge framed poster of Joe Montana (the quarterback of the San Francisco 49'ers). There were framed pictures of the LA Lakers and a signed basketball from Magic Johnson. Warden Dennis was a huge sports fan and attended many live events up and down the state. He was also a huge fan of the rodeo. He would go to Sacramento every year for the state rodeo championships and would go to Texas for the national championships. Boxing, however, was the warden's first love. Sugar Ray Robinson was his all-time favorite fighter. He was a regular at the boxing matches in Oakland and San Francisco. He would also attend the monthly matches in Los Angeles. Warden Dennis was overly excited that Leonard had the potential to put PSP on the map. Little did Leonard know just how excited Warden Dennis really was.

"Leonard please have a seat. Do you like the office?" The Warden asked.

"Yes I do Warden Dennis." Leonard said kindly.

"Leonard everyone here is looking forward to you going for the CPBA welterweight title. As you know I'm a huge boxing fan. I loved the sport since I was a little kid. There is an art to a man hitting and not getting hit. I saw your first fight at Fulton and knew that you had potential."

"I didn't know you were there Warden Dennis?" Leonard surprisingly replied.

"Yes I never miss the state fights. I sat in a special seat as to not be recognized. But trust me I saw every minute of the fights that night. I've seen all seven of your fights. I had CB in my office last week and told him how fond I was of you. I know that you've been a model citizen since you've been here and now you're on the cusp of winning a title. You are building up some good karma here at PSP. I'll tell you this. You are up for parole in 3 years. I want in the worst way for PSP to be the # 1 boxing team in the CPBA. Leonard, if you win the title I can guarantee that you will be paroled in '93. I don't want to put any extra pressure on you, look at it more like extra incentive for you to win the title. There will be no penalty for you not winning. I'm going to support you either way. Leonard you have the chance to do something really huge here and totally turn your life around."

"Warden, thanks for vote of confidence. I am looking forward to '93. You can get the paperwork ready because I'll be winning the CPBA title.

"Leonard I have faith in you and can't wait for the celebration. If you win the title I'll make sure you get a meal from the outside in your cell."

Warden Dennis got up and signaled for the guard to escort Leonard back to his cell. They shook hands and Warden Dennis again assured Leonard that he had his full support. Leonard's brain was racing! The promise of parole was icing on the cake. Leonard already wanted the CPBA title in the worst way, but now the incentive of automatic parole was the ultimate motivation. Although Leonard was on the boxing team and had some clout around the institution, he still was in a small cell every night. He was still inside of a steel gate 45 miles from Oakland. Those 45 miles seemed like he was in Utah. The boxing team lightened the mode of survival in PSP but it wasn't freedom. Freedom was based on winning the title in '89. Leonard was thinking of all those things on his way back to the cell. Once inside the cell he looked at his pictures and whispered out loud "we're out of here in '93!"

It felt like years but the prison-boxing tournament was only a few weeks away. He was ready for the welterweight tournament. He was feeling good and fit. 7 KO's in 7 fights and his name was ringing bells up and down the west coast prison system. CB was receiving letters from some of his people back down in LA and they were asking about who this kid Leonard was. Leonard heard that people were talking about him but he remained grounded. CB kept him focused and Leonard knew what was at stake. He was fighting for himself, CB, PSP and most importantly his freedom. That freedom meant everything to Leonard and to be the CPBA version of Marvelous Marvin Hearns.

"Leonard, to be champ means that all of your hard work is validated. Hearns, Ali, Pryor, and all of the other champs represented the championship and they worked extra hard to get it and maintain it. You have everything it takes to get there. When, not if, you win the title, the first thing you should be grateful for is the fact that your hard work paid off. A man doesn't know what he can do until he really puts in the work. Your physical work is done in the dungeon but your mental work never ends. It's a constant routine of sharpening your mental axe. When you win this title I'll be the happiest man in the world. 1989 is the year that you step up and let the state know that you're the toughest dude in the system. This is about legacy. This is about representing for you. Win this title for you Leonard. Not for me, not for the warden, not for PSP, win this for you. You will be a 20-year-old welterweight champion! Let that soak in and replay it in your mind over and over until that final bell rings and they put that belt around your waist."

Three weeks in PSP could crawl by. Anyone that has ever been incarcerated will tell you that prison time crawls by much slower than time on the outside. Prison time is the definition of redundancy. A lot of inmates talk the same shit day after day. A west coast tradition is playing the game of dominoes. Dominoes reigned supreme at PSP. It was so big that they had tournaments to determine who the best was at PSP. It was the number one pastime for inmates to keep them occupied. Some inmates that think they are getting paroled mark of each day on a calendar in their cell. Others try not to talk about it and stay busy exercising or reading. Some take classes to get their General Equivalency Diploma. For Leonard, time was crawling by extra slow. His anxiety level was at an all-time high and he was having trouble containing his nervous energy. Being CPBA champion and automatic parole dominated his thinking. He couldn't, for good reason, think of anything else. He tried the meditation techniques that CB suggested but they didn't work. His desire to accomplish his major goals outweighed whatever else was going on in the world. Leonard had no idea what was going on in the outside world. All he was focused on was CPBA champ and '93. He knew once he won the title he wouldn't lose it. He knew that he would be released in '93 and maybe become a professional boxer. The time would come for him to display his discipline to the state of California.

With focus and intensity the outcome was never in doubt! Leonard won the CPBA welterweight title in grand fashion. Just like his first fight with Grady, Leonard won the title with a knockout. The fight only lasted 91 seconds, like Tyson's fight with Spinks, and the prison crowd went crazy. Leonard dropped to his knees and thanked his creator. CB held back tears in the middle of the ring and Warden Dennis jumped in the ring after the fight to congratulate Leonard. The boxing team carried Leonard around the ring and Leonard pumped his fist in jubilation. Excitement was an understatement. Leonard thought of Hearns and how he lost to Sugar Ray back in '81. Many accused Hearns of not being aggressive enough during that fight. Leonard wasn't going to let his fight go to the judges. Many days and nights of contemplating the fight had paid off in a big way. CB knew that Leonard would win but he always nervous until the fight was officially over. CB knew that Leonard was the best fighter in the California Prison System regardless of weight. Leonard was a special talent and this was his moment. Leonard was the toast of the town. All of the prison dignitaries were there to congratulate Leonard on his victory. Leonard Smith had made it from the juvenile detention centers from Oakland to a California prison-boxing champion. Never in his wildest dreams could Leonard have imagined that he would be boxing or be a champion. Now he was both and his goals were obtained.

"Warden Dennis I would like a double cheeseburger, Fries, 6 piece Nugget and a chocolate shake from McDonalds." Leonard said with liberation.

"Leonard you got it. You deserve it and I'm a man of my word. You'll be able to eat plenty of that in 3 years. Parole for you is coming!" The warden said.

"Warden I will continue to represent for PSP. My career is just getting started."

"I'm looking forward to many more victories from you. Everyone up and down the coast is talking about how special you are."

"CB gets all the credit for this victory! If it wasn't for him I'd be dead or doing life." Leonard replied.

"CB will also get a meal and you both can eat in my office. Enjoy this victory and we'll eat tomorrow. "Leonard and CB enjoyed the meal and reveled in the victory and having the ability to eat in the Warden's office. CB accomplished what he set out when he first saw Leonard knock Bone out in the mess hall. CB could now retire if he wanted to but CB wanted to go on the 3 year ride with Leonard.

Release,

Leonard went 4 years undefeated at PSP. 33-0 and defended the welterweight title the entire time. Leonard Smith was only the second fighter in the history of the CPBA to go undefeated. It was a great accomplishment because there were many top tier fighters in his division. CB wanted Leonard to fight Raul Marquez. Marquez represented the 1992 U.S. Olympic Boxing Team at 156 pounds. CB wrote letters to set up the fight, as did the Warden, but the International Olympic Committee (IOC) wouldn't let Marquez fight an unsanctioned fight. The IOC didn't have insurance coverage for amateur athletes to fight in a state prison bout. Marquez wasn't a professional and therefore was still under the guise of the IOC. The fight would've been a huge deal for the CPBA but it never came to fruition.

Leonard gained the attention of many promoters up and down the west coast. Warden Dennis had allowed a few to come to PSP and speak to Leonard and CB. Many of the promoters and boxing managers came to the CPBA fights so they were familiar with Leonard Smith. Leonard intended to turn professional when he was paroled. CB was helping him figure out his next move. His hometown of Oakland was beginning to develop a reputation for boxing. Quite a few gyms had opened up in Oakland and also across the bridge in San Francisco. The hotbed for boxing in California was Los Angeles. The newest "it" boxer was '92 Olympian Oscar De La Hoya. He won the gold medal as a lightweight and was nicknamed "The Golden Boy." He was being promoted as the new face of boxing. The 80's were over and former Heavyweight Champ Mike Tyson was in prison in Indiana on a rape conviction. All eyes were on the LA boxing scene and The Golden Boy.

CB knew that eventually Leonard would have to make his bones on the LA boxing scene. He was already behind in terms of turning professional. Most guys with his talent turn pro at 19 or 20. Because of his prison stint he wouldn't be turning pro until 23. His prison experience counted as his amateur record. No better experience to have then against the toughest dudes in California. Ultimately it would be Leonard's decision as to where he wanted to begin his career. Oakland offered Leonard an opportunity to spar with some tough competition and it was 20 minutes from San Francisco. The bay area is a 5-hour drive to LA so he had to decide between the two. CB presented Leonard with all options and gave him the pros and cons of his decision.

CB felt like a proud poppa and was ambivalent about Leonard being paroled. He was happy for Leonard but was sad that he was leaving. The past five years were the best years of CB's life. Leonard had been his star pupil and was like a son to him. His feelings for Leonard extended beyond boxing. CB was thankful that Leonard put the PSP boxing team on the map. CB attributed Leonard's success to his willingness to be coached. CB was selfish in the fact that he wanted Leonard to stay. CB's life was all about boxing and now there would be a huge void that could never be filled. CB was a lifer with no chance for parole. His life was Leonard. All that he had become was centered on the development of Leonard Smith. CB looked at Leonard like the son he would never have. Leonard being paroled also reminded CB of his life sentence without the possibility of parole. CB was now in his 40's and was totally different from the man that committed the crime that landed him in PSP. No matter how much he changed or how much he contributed to the PSP boxing team, his life would be spent at PSP. There was no separate penthouse suite at PSP. There was no special elevator that took CB up and down to the dungeon. Leonard's release put his own life into perspective. CB realized his own situation.

During the five year run with Leonard, CB was able to take his mind off of his life without parole. The concrete walls and lowlife inmates were the reality for CB. The irony is that CB saved

Leonard's life but couldn't save his own. CB had the respect of every inmate at PSP. That respect didn't mean anything in society. CB was a model inmate and had become a model citizen. He was an avid reader and instilled discipline and life lessons into the PSP boxing team. He poured all that he had into Leonard. The lessons worked for Leonard while he was at PSP. Could those lessons translate out in society? CB knew that the recidivism rate was high in the California prison system. The rate was especially high at PSP because the level of criminality was intense. Most guys that got paroled didn't have the social skills to survive in a positive manner in society. There was no rehabilitation in prison. The streets didn't offer the structure that prison did. There was a head count three times a day at PSP. Inmates had accountability and the threat of the hole and more time if they missed a head count. For lifers the threat was being transferred to a maximum-security prison where they would be in their cells 23 hours a day. CB feared that Leonard could be pulled back in the allure of the streets. With all of the discipline Leonard had developed, he still had no stable environment. CB hadn't talked to Leonard about the pitfalls of the streets but that talk was coming.

"Leonard I'm a man of my word and your release is upon us. In 3 days you'll be gone. I appreciate you putting the PSP boxing team on the map. Hopefully you'll stay out of trouble."

With those words Warden Dennis shook Leonard's hand. Leonard left the Warden's office. Now it was finally hitting Leonard that he was leaving PSP. Leonard hadn't thought a lot about leaving PSP. The thought of leaving created confusion in Leonard's mind. Leonard thought back to '88 and his intake process. He remembered lying on his cot and wondering if he would ever survive in this hell- hole. Playing the early days over in his head, Leonard thought about being 17, scared, and crying in his pillow. Leonard thought about the first day when he had to walk through the mess hall and was shaking in his sneakers. Darkness is what PSP meant to him in those early days. In those early days he knew that it was kill or be killed. Leonard was prepared to kill someone if he had to. Fortunately that didn't happen. Leonard became a killer but it wasn't in a murderous sense. Leonard was walking back to his cell and staring straight ahead. He didn't notice another human being.

Leonard was a little indifferent about his release. From the first day he arrived at PSP, all he thought about was getting back to Oakland. Now that the time was here Leonard didn't know how to feel. He was ready for a real bed and some real food. Leonard wanted some Chinese food and a cold soda. He wanted a burger from In-N-Out out near the coliseum. He wanted to go to a Raiders game and boo the Broncos, Chiefs, and Chargers. He wanted to go to the skate palace in downtown Oakland. He wanted to ride the BART and go to the mission district in San Francisco. All of the things he wanted to do would become a reality in a few days.

The Warden made sure that the boxing team got paid for their fights. In PSP being part of the boxing team equaled having a job. Leonard had $4,000 in his account that he would be taking with him when he left. Leonard missed his late teen years and the first three years of his 20's. Leonard had developed a lot of discipline being on the boxing team. CB had saved and changed his life at PSP. Leonard was now an avid reader of books and a student of boxing. On the surface it would seem that Leonard was well equipped to handle himself back on the streets of Oakland. In five years, Leonard had barely talked to any of his homies in Oakland. He corresponded with his siblings but they only came to visit a few times. Leonard didn't want them to come to see him at PSP. They saw him fight when he fought outside of San Jose. Leonard needed to reconnect with his father. Leonard wasn't sure what would happen to him when he got back to the streets. PSP was a dangerous place but after he joined the boxing team Leonard felt a level of safety. Leonard never had that feeling of safety in East Oakland. His violent behavior was a result of him fearing for his life and he was a wolf not a sheep.

Leonard was ready for change. Leonard wanted a different life back on the streets. He had to get with a manager and begin his professional boxing career. CB still wanted him to go to LA but Leonard wanted to start his career at home in Oakland. LA always seemed like another world to Leonard. The bay area was totally separate from Southern California. The rivalry between Northern and Southern California was very real. Some say the bay area was jealous of LA. The bay area residents thought that people in the LA area were very pretentious and soft. Perception can become reality. Leonard didn't have a problem with people from LA. Many of the inmates were from LA as was CB. Leonard just wanted that hometown feeling of being back in Oakland. Leonard understood that he had to start boxing right away. He had met a few cats from other parts of Oakland that said they would keep in touch on the outside. Leonard was going to reach out to them to see what type of connections they had. Leonard was itching to leave his cell and he only had seventy two hours left.

He imagined what a bedroom would feel like. When he left he had plans to move with his older sister Alicia. Alicia had a small 3-bedroom house on Olive Street right off of Bancroft Street in East Oakland. Alicia mailed him pictures of her house and it looked like a mansion compared to his cell. Leonard would have his own room. Alicia worked for the city of Oakland as a receptionist. She had a boyfriend and no kids. Leonard told her that he was only going to stay for a few months and then get his own apartment. Leonard was hoping to get a job near a boxing gym so he could walk back and forth between work and the gym. Leonard was going to spend his money on boxing equipment and getting some clothes to wear to a job interview. Leonard figured he would have to work until he could start making money as a professional boxer. That was his goal. He wanted the money that Tyson and Oscar De La Hoya were getting for their fights. He knew that it would take hard work but eventually he would get there.

An 8x10 cell is all he knew for the last 5 years. Every night at 9:00 pm the cell gates would close and wouldn't open until 6:30 am. Unless it was an emergency you were locked in that cell for nine straight hours. Some men couldn't handle it and were found dangling from the ceiling in the morning. Leonard never thought about killing himself but there were many long nights contemplating the meaning of life. This night was different from the past 1,824 nights. This night would be his last at PSP. Leonard knew that he would barely be able to sleep due to the anxiety but he was going to try. He took down his pictures of Hearns and Aaron Pryor. He was going to give CB all of his books and magazines back. He wanted CB to have the pictures of Hearns.

Once he got his own apartment Leonard was going to put up pictures of him winning fights and newspaper clippings that would write about his achievements. Everything that reminded him of PSP he would leave there. In his mind it was a fresh start. He would treat the streets with more respect. Unlike when he was 17, Leonard now understood what it was like to do hard time. He understood the how valuable freedom was and he wasn't going to lose that again. Being locked up in a California state penitentiary was no place for anyone much less a seventeen-year old juvenile.

July 12th 1993 was like any other day in PSP. The slop breakfast was being served and the shit talking started early in the morning. Dominoes, cards, and lifting weights had already begun in the prison yard. CB was where he always was, in the dungeon with the team. Leonard was late this morning because he was finishing an exit interview with the prison psychologist. It was required for every inmate that was being paroled. It would stay in his file and a copy would be given to his parole officer along with any incident report that may have occurred while he was at PSP. He also received his bus ticket. PSP had arrangements with BART to transport inmates back to their respective neighborhoods (those that didn't have someone to pick them up). Leonard finally made it to the dungeon and for the first time in a long time he became overwhelmed with emotion.

He stared at the fight posters. Those fights posters were the first thing Leonard remembered seeing when he entered the dungeon five years ago. He envisioned being on one of those posters one day and now it was possible. He stared at the floor and the ring. This makeshift boxing gym had literally saved his life. These old ropes and that old heavy bag had been his ticket to staying alive during his 60-month stint at PSP. The dungeon was the place that became his safe haven. It was the place that Leonard called home. The dungeon allowed Leonard to work through all of his family issues and concentrate on becoming a better young man. The dungeon was the escape from the horrific realities that were upstairs in the general population of PSP. PSP had one of the highest homicide rates among prisons in the state of California. The dungeon was the one place that Leonard felt free to express his talents. On the streets of Oakland Leonard didn't know that he had any special talent. The only talent he had was creating chaos and havoc. When he walked in the dungeon Leonard could hear the floors creak under the weight of his steps. Leonard relished in the dust kicking up from the rope being jumped and as fate would have it, Leonard was about to embark on saying goodbye to CB.

CB noticed Leonard walking around the dungeon. CB, much like Leonard, was very melancholy about his star pupil leaving. CB knew that the PSP boxing team would never be the same. Raw boxers like Leonard don't come around very often. CB became the most popular trainer in the CPBA system because of Leonard. And Leonard's life was saved because of this old-head from South Central Los Angeles.

"This is where the magic happened, Leonard." CB said nostalgically.

"CB this was it. This old rusty place saved my life!" Leonard replied.

"Leonard, always remember this place. This place can make boys into men or reduce men to boys. A lot of cats walking around PSP like they're tough but if you bring them down here and put gloves on them they would fold like a cheap tent. This separates the men from the boys. Boxing is the one sport where there is no timeout. In the ring it's just you and your opponent. That's the beauty of the sport. I love it because if you're not thinking you can get hurt; this is why I preach focus, stamina, and defense."

"The dungeon is where my life began to take shape."

"Leonard this is a huge step in your life. Most of the dudes here will never get out. You have a chance to make everything you did wrong, right. The boxing team was a chance for you to see a different side of life. However as dangerous as PSP is, the streets are far more dangerous. Once you get adjusted to how prison life works it's easy to adapt and look out for the pitfalls. On the streets there is no way to adapt. The streets are always changing. I've been here since the mid 60's and the world has changed but the streets haven't. Just listen to the stories of the new guys that get booked. Shit has changed but the meaning of the streets is the same. I want you to always be mindful of how the streets operate. The streets take no prisoners. The concrete jungle will eat you up.

Boxing can be your savior. Boxing can be the way you avoid the dangers of East Oakland. Whether you stay in Oakland, go down to LA, or fly to New York; the issues will be the same. You've come too far to go back to how you were in the 80's. The only place you'll end up is back here or in Pelican Bay on 23- hour lockdown. The next time I want to see your face is in Ring Magazine."

"CB, the next time I want to see you is on a visit. I wish you could go out and be my trainer and manager on the outside. I owe you my life! I never plan on going back to the way I was in the 80's. I want to build on everything I read and everything you taught me."

"Leonard you gave this whole team pride. Embody the spirit of Malcolm X on the outside. Discipline is the key to success. Nothing is gained in life without hard work. Make me proud out there Leonard Smith."

"I plan on it CB!" Conrad gave Leonard a piece of paper with a name and number on it, Wade Taylor (510) 251-6587.

"Leonard this is an old friend and a brilliant boxing man. His gym is on E 14th Street in your part of town. Look him up and he will take care of you like I did."

After that exchange the teacher and the pupil embraced. There were tears in the eyes of the two men who had become attached at the hip for the past 5 years. They both knew that life wouldn't be the same after this moment. Leonard gave CB all of the pictures, magazines and books that he had in his cell. Leonard also embraced each member of the team and took one last look at the dungeon. He shook his head in acknowledgement of what the dungeon represented and headed back to his cell to gather his belongings. Leonard took his last look at the 8x10 box that was his living quarters since 1988.

Leonard was escorted through PSP out to the entrance of the facility. There was a bus at the front gate. Leonard was the only inmate being discharged from PSP. As the gates opened Leonard looked back one last time at the immense structure known as PSP. Leonard took one last look at the armed guard in the guard shack above the yard. The bus doors swung open and Leonard walked up and greeted the bus driver. Leonard had a bag with him with his money and some regular clothes. The guard wished Leonard luck and shook his hand. Leonard knew that he never wanted to come back to PSP, except to visit CB, but Leonard had no idea what the streets had in store for him. The bus driver closed the door and the bus was headed down I-80 headed for I-880 and the Bus Depot at the Oakland Coliseum.

Part 2

1986 - 1988

Chapter 11
Background,

"Let me tell you something. I'll knock you the fuck out right here on the ave. I don't give a fuck who your crew is. I don't give a fuck who the leader of your crew is. I'll beat all y'all the fuck up. You been up here poppin' fly the past two weeks. James fucked your bitch and it ain't shit you can do about it. James got popped night before last and we out here reppin' his name. This ain't your side of town. You can pop that shit over by Fruitvale or in Lake Merritt but here in East Oakland, your ass is mine. I don't know whether to beat your ass, pistol whip you or let my dog eat your ass. Time is up on all that bullshit you been talking." "Marco I told you to pipe the fuck down and you didn't want to listen. That Superman cape is about to be burned!"

Leonard Smith was as violent a teenager that you could find in all of California. He was only 16 but already graduated from the school of hard knocks. Shit he had a PHD in street life. He had no regard for human life. It was amazing that he was still alive. He was born in 1970 in East Oakland, California, to a father who was a down on his luck gambler and a mother who drifted in and out of consciousness due to her heroin addiction. Leonard and his two sisters basically raised themselves. They had the sanctuary of their Grandparents house in nearby Hayward, which was only a few miles away but it felt like it was as far away as New York City.

Being raised in a dysfunctional household had the same effect on Leonard that it had on a lot of other inner city kids, he was fucked up. The nurturing he was supposed to receive at an early stage in life was replaced with runs to the corner store to buy beer and cigarettes. I love you was replaced with "Why the fuck are you crying?" There were times when Leonard was a baby and his diaper wouldn't be changed for days. Leonard's dad tried to hold things together. He worked two jobs and kept food in the house but was gone most of the time rolling dice, drinking beer, and playing cards. They used to have a card game at the house every Thursday night but Leonard's dad was too much in debt and had to stop the game until he paid his debts. If he didn't pay his debts he would've been shot at the next game.

Leonard's parents were born and raised in Oakland. They got married young and had big dreams like a lot of young couples. Leonard's dad, Marvin, got a job right out of high school as a construction worker with the city of Oakland. His mom, Arlene, went to college for a year right after high school. She dropped out after she became pregnant with Leonard's oldest sister Alicia. Marvin got the family a two-bedroom house and life was good in the Smith household. Marvin and Arlene were a young couple in love and happy to be starting a family. By the time Leonard was born things had changed drastically in the house. The free flowing party ways of the 1960's had caught up to the Smiths and Leonard was born right in the middle of the madness.

It started going downhill in late 1968. Marvin was hosting a card party listening to some Motown music, drinking beer, and eating snacks. Up to that point Arlene rarely played cards with Marvin. She would stay in the other room with the girls and out of the way of the guys. This particular night the girls were with Arlene's parents. The fellas came over around 8:30pm and the card party started. One of Marvin's friends, Joey, brought his girlfriend Mia with him. Mia and Joey were a wild couple that liked to party and have a good time. Arlene had met Mia before and liked her a little bit. Mia didn't have kids yet but she and Arlene were the same age. They began to small talk and sip on some vodka and orange juice while the fellas played cards. Arlene and Mia danced to the music and drank half a bottle of vodka together. Joey stepped away from the card game and joined Mia and Arlene.

Joey said to Arlene "Looks like you're really ready to party?"

"Yeah I haven't had fun like this in a long time. "Arlene replied.

"Good I'm glad Mia could help you relax. I have something that can really help you relax. That vodka is cool but this bag right here will make you forget about the world." Joey had a bag of heroin. He called it the "party starter" & the heroin was fresh from New York. It was a bag of the pure stuff. Joey's cousin was a drug dealer from New York. He moved to California to expand his drug business. Joey would get free dope because he would always provide his cousin with new customers. The dope that Joey had was some of the best in the country. Joey made sure that Marvin was engrossed in the card game. He bought him a couple of beers so that he would be occupied and needing to go to the bathroom. Joey knew that once Arlene got a taste of this heroin, she would be hooked. Joey was a slimy dude that only cared about himself. Arlene would be another customer for his cousin and more free dope for Joey. Joey didn't care how this would affect Marvin and his family; he just cared about the dope.

"This here starts the party and ends the party at the same damn time. Me & Mia use this to keep it live at the crib. You and Marv already got it going on baby and now this bag will always keep y'all happy. Trust me baby!"

"I'm ready to party." Arlene shouted. With that statement Joey and Arlene both put dollar bills to their noses and sniffed the party starter. Arlene's eyes rolled back in her head and her body jerked and twitched. Euphoria enveloped her mind, body and soul. She had never had a feeling like that ever in her life. Her body wasn't yet ready to respond but her mind wanted more of the party starter. Joey smiled and kissed Arlene on the forehead. After 15 minutes Arlene was still fucked up but ready for more. For the next hour Arlene sniffed plenty of the party starter. She went in and out of consciousness all night. Before the card game was over Joey and Mia left. No need to have a confrontation with Marvin, plus Joey knew that Arlene would be calling him very soon.

Arlene never recovered from that night. Marvin tried to get her clean and sober but it would only work for short periods of time. Every time she stayed clean for a few months, she would always dip back into it. Marvin never touched the heroin but

Arlene's addiction caused him to drink more and more and soon he was a full-fledged alcoholic. He stayed away from the house because he felt pity and rage towards his wife. His kids suffered because his parents were in complete dysfunction. The Smith child that suffered the most was Leonard.

Leonard and Todd tied Marco's hands behind his back. They proceeded to pistol whip him and kick him in his face for the next 10 minutes. They didn't kill him because they wanted his face to be a warning to anyone else that talked shit on the Ave Crew. (Leonard, Todd and James called themselves the Ave Crew because they were always on the Avenue. Before their teenage years began, they were on the streets playing basketball and football. But now the crime element had taken over their DNA). Marco begged for mercy but Leonard and Todd didn't want to hear shit. At this point Marco's life was hanging in the balance. Neither Todd nor Leonard was very level headed but they knew that it was better to keep Marco alive then face a murder rap. Marco wouldn't snitch because the Ave Crew would kill him. The beef started after James fucked Marco's girl. Marco was telling everyone who listened that he was going to fuck James up and anyone who was with him. Before they beat his ass, Leonard made sure word got back to Marco that if he stepped on the East side of Oakland, his ass was grass. This is how Leonard handled beefs on the street. It wasn't the first time Leonard pistol-whipped somebody. But this time it was more viscous. They fucked Marco up real good! Marco could barely walk. Todd & Leonard got one of their women to drive Marco back to his turf. Marco was lured to East Oakland by a chick that Leonard fucks on the side. They sent her to a local hangout where they knew Marco would be. She enticed him to give her a ride back near Bancroft and when he stopped there Leonard and Todd were there to snatch him out of the car. Marco never saw Leonard or the 9mm he put to his temple.

Leonard and Todd didn't know when something else would happen, but they knew that this wasn't the end of the beef. Beefs like this only end when someone dies. James was locked up so Leonard and Todd had to represent for the crew. Rules of the streets dictated that they do whatever they had to do to make sure they remained in power. The *King of Jungle* philosophy was always at the forefront of street action. It was kill or be killed. There was no time for diplomacy on the streets. The streets don't sleep. The streets are always watching and people know when it's time to make a move. Marco wouldn't let a beating like that go without payback. Leonard and Todd were now marked men until James came out of lock up and could handle the situation himself. Teenagers don't often think about the ramifications of what their actions. In their minds, they did what they had to do. Street cred was everything and whatever happened after that didn't matter.

Leonard lived that life. He was street smart and had no regard for his own existence. Leonard couldn't think about the future because he knew that any day could be his last. It's hard to grasp the concepts of love and forgiveness when your parents are drug and alcohol abusers. Love comes from your friends and the respect you earn on the concrete. Many inner city youth, especially on the west coast, dealt with life and death situations on a daily basis. Gang life in California in the 80's was much more prevalent than on the East Coast. Gangs gave a lot of youth on the streets a sense of belonging. Many, like Leonard, came from broken homes. They had no role models. They didn't have positive male figures to discuss with them and teach them what manhood was all about. The gangs were the teachers. The gang leaders became the mothers and fathers for all the wayward young teenagers. Leonard's crew wasn't considered a gang. They functioned as a small time crime unit and leaned on each other. Leonard knew that if he officially joined a gang it would be impossible to get out. The only way out of a gang was death. Leonard was young but the streets smarts he had made him wise beyond his years. The gang life would give him a lifetime contract to the streets. Although Leonard had no plans for the rest of his life, he knew that the gangs would eat him alive. A lot of the gang life was still centered in Southern California but Oakland was starting to get an influx of the gang life and all the people Leonard's age were being recruited. Leonard refused to be recruited.

Leonard and Todd agreed that they would lay low for a few days. Marco would tell his crew what happened and they might come around to the ave looking for trouble. Marco's crew also knew that Marco was asking for an ass whipping by always talking shit. Leonard went down to his cousin's house in Hayward. His cousin Charles rolled with the Ave Crew whenever he came up to Oakland. Charles wasn't as bad as Leonard but he was no angel either. Charles' father was doing 25 to life in Pelican Bay for attempted murder. Charles was dealing crack on a small level. Hayward wasn't as volatile as Oakland. Charles knew it was trouble when he saw Leonard at his door.

"Leonard what's up cuz?"

"Charles, my big cuz, what's popping? I got into hella shit on the Ave and I need to cool out for a few days. You think Aunt Roslyn will let me cool out for a few days?"

"Yeah man my mom is working two jobs right now. She might not even know you're here and if she did she would love to see you."

"Cool. I'll chill out for a few days until the heat dies down a little. Those niggas that roll with Marco might be hot for a few days but they be into so much shit, they'll be onto something else in soon. I'm only chilling because Todd has a little one on the way and don't need that bullshit. You know me cuz I'll fuck anyone of those niggas up but me and Todd roll thick so we a package deal. I can't have Todd getting plucked with a baby on the way. The streets don't care about his baby. A punk ass bitch like Marco would love to ruin Todd's life right now. We need James to get out and handle this for himself. Right now we riding for him but this is some bullshit. "

"L you know I'm down for you so you just say the word and I'll be on the Ave ready to put in some work. Plus I got cousins on my dad's side from LA that bang hard and would come up to the bay for a price."

"Nah Charles it ain't that deep. We'll save the LA cats for when we really need them. Marco and his crew are bitch ass dudes and don't really want that work. Any girls to play with down here in Hayward?"

"Yeah man I'll make a phone call. I have this bitch Candy that that will suck and fuck both of us. You ever pull a train?"

"Nah but I'm ready to. Let's get a couple of 40's and see what we can do with this bitch. I need some pussy. Cousin Charles making it happen! I appreciate you man. Let's go get some cold Old English and have some fun."

They went to the corner store and got four 40's of Old English 800 (Ole E). For two teenagers, that was plenty of malt liquor to get them ready to sexually abuse a female. Charles had a fake ID and a beard so getting beer wasn't a problem. Charles also got a couple of wine coolers for Candy. Candy wasn't an official prostitute but Charles gave her money if he had it. Leonard typically never exchanged money for sex, however he told Charles he would take care of Candy. Charles and Leonard blasted some Eric B & Rakim and some Ice T and drank one 40 in about 10 minutes. The faster you drank malt liquor the more of a buzz you got. Drinking that first one had Leonard's head spinning. He was dancing and trying to do his own raps. They pretended to be Run DMC and passed the empty 40 bottle to each other like a microphone. At that moment Leonard was in a state of euphoria. He wasn't thinking about how fucked up his parents were. He wasn't thinking about the current assault charges he had on him and the fact that he had to go to court and probably juvenile detention next month. He wasn't thinking about Marco and that bullshit. He was enjoying spending time with his cousin and looking forward to having some teenage sex.

Leonard looked around and was in awe of his Aunt's home. Leonard wasn't used to seeing family pictures on the wall. Leonard's parents barely had running water. His father paid the bills when he could but most of his money went to alcohol and gambling. Leonard paid some bills because he needed somewhere to sleep and he wanted to make sure that his sisters functioned well during the day at school. He wanted them to make something of their lives. He knew his was going to be fucked up but he had dreams for his sisters. The smell of his Aunt's house struck Leonard. He could feel the love and hard work she had. The house was clean and they had food in the kitchen. He looked at Charles and through his alcoholic stupor he had a moment of clarity. He told Charles to call Candy and tell her not to come over.

"Leonard are you too drunk?"

"Nah cuz. I can't disrespect Aunt Rosalyn. She's like a mom to me, shit she's more mom than my own. I'm looking around and she's at work right now and she does right by y'all. I wish she was my real mom. Man this house is too nice for some dumb shit. Charles you got a chance. Man, fuck the streets where I'm at. You can do some other shit. Aunt Rosalyn is better than my parents. Damn this 40 got me seeing shit clear. Now me I'm staying in the game but you, it's time for you to break out and get right."

"Leonard, you trippin."

"Nah bro I'm serious. I'm headed outta here and back to Oakland. I'm going to jump on the BART. I'll check out Drew and Wayne over in Lake Merritt and chill with them for a few days. I'll be cool. Charles just remember what I said. Stay off these streets. Get a job and push it down to LA, that's the move for you.

"Leonard, I hear you. Stay up cousin."

"I'll check you later Charles. Tell Aunt Rosalyn I said hi and I'll come visit next weekend."

"Cool."

Leonard sat on the BART and sobered up. He thought long and hard about what he said to Charles. He wished that he could actually take his own advice. He knew the only way for him to leave the streets was to move to LA but he was Oakland all the way. He wasn't mature enough nor did he have the resources to make a move like that. The petty shit that the Ave crew did made some money but LA was another world. Besides in his mind it was just a matter of time until he was King on Oakland, at least in East Oakland. With each BART stop he started to think more and more about his mom. Seeing pictures of Aunt Rosalyn, his father's sister, made him long for a beautiful mother like that. He began daydreaming about his mom being like Claire Huxtable from the Cosby Show. Every Thursday he went to Todd's house and watched the Cosby Show. It seemed like every black person in America in 1986 watched that show. He knew his mom wasn't anything more than a heroin addict. Even at 16 soon to be 17 he wasn't disillusioned about who his mom really was. His mom was never going to be shit but a junkie. It was amazing she lived this long. Leonard despised his parents and thought they were weak. He promised himself that if he ever had a family he would be a good dad and make sure his wife never used drugs.

Chapter 12
1988

Arlene had been in this house before. It was a dingy dilapidated house in the Eastmont neighborhood in East Oakland. Everyone on the block knew that this house was a notorious drug house. Like most cities in the 80's, Oakland felt the ravages of the crack epidemic. Crack replaced the feel good drugs of the 70's like cocaine and marijuana. Crack was cheaper than all the other drugs and easy to make. People like Arlene did whatever she could to get high. It didn't matter to her whether it was crack or heroin but heroin was still her drug of choice. Her veins were almost gone from all the drug abuse over the years. She was unrecognizable to people that hadn't seen her in years. She weighed less than 100 pounds and looked way beyond her 40 years of age. She went from a mother and wife to a street addict. She rarely slept at their house. Marvin gave up on ever having a marriage. He, like Leonard, accepted the fact that Arlene was married and loyal to the drugs.

The house in Eastmont was dark with a flickering lamp in the corner. There were a few junkies in the house and Mark the local drug dealer. Arlene was with her drug partner, Denise. Denise had the same type of story as Arlene. She got hooked at an early age and could never kick the habit. Her family left her in Oakland and moved down to LA. They wanted nothing to do with her and totally disowned her. Arlene and Denise both did whatever they had to do to get drugs. This night they both sucked Mark's dick. Mark was a young boy and he loved the tricks because they would suck and fuck him every day. He had other paying customers that kept money in his pocket. Tricks like Denise and Arlene fulfilled his sexual desires. Arlene had just finished sucking his dick in the basement. For that he gave her a bag of raw heroin that would keep her and Denise high for the rest of the night. It was 11:30 pm and the night was just getting started. The ladies couldn't wait for the heroin to hit their veins. They had gone quite a few hours with no dope and they were now fiendin'. The dope kept them alive and killed them at the same time. They were already missing most of their teeth and hadn't showered in days. Hygiene didn't matter to them; the only thing that mattered to them was getting high. For Arlene it had been this way since that card game back in 1968. Most people didn't make it this long in the drug game but for whatever reason Arlene was still hanging in there. Most addicts never think about their mortality. Rational thinking doesn't equate to junkies. It never has and never will.

"Girl I'm glad you sucked Mark off in the basement. I'll be getting some money tomorrow. They still give me SSI money for my dad. I have to go to the social security place every 15th of the month. I take the BART downtown, sign some paperwork and get a check. I'll cash it on International and we can leave Mark alone for a few days. We can go get that real shit over in Seminary."

"Yeah that's the plan. Tie my arm up real tight"

"Arlene you gonna have to start putting this in between your toes. Girl your arm veins are gone."

"Alright tomorrow. Let's use this last good vein tonight!"

Denise placed the needle in Arlene's arm like she did many times before. She shot the raw heroin through Arlene's veins and Arlene's eyes rolled in the back of her head. For 2 minutes she had her head laid back on the couch. She drooped over and her head swayed from side to side. She slid off the couch and fell to the floor. She was on her left side and foam was coming out of her mouth. She was twitching and her body was shaking violently. Denise didn't know what to do. She couldn't call 911; they were in a drug house. She yelled for Mark and he came running in from the kitchen.

"What the fuck happened to her?" he yelled.

"She shot up 2 minutes ago and ended up on the floor." Denise screamed.

"Damn. That raw is strong. I'm gonna have to cut that a little bit."

"What should we do with her?" Denise frantically yelled.

"Fuck if I know? Let's throw some cold water on her. Maybe she'll wake up." Mark said carelessly.

Mark filled up a pot of cold water. He threw it directly in Arlene's face. Arlene didn't move. Denise yelled her name and Arlene didn't respond. The other junkies saw what was going on and ran out the back. Mark threw another pot of water on her and nothing.

"This bitch is dead!"

"No, she can't be. She was just on the couch."

"I'm telling you she gone. We can't leave her here. Fuck! I gotta dump her in an alley somewhere."

"We can't do that. We have to take her to the hospital."

"And what the fuck we supposed to tell em? Huh? Umm she was shooting heroin and stopped moving so we brought her here. That's dumb. We'll both get locked up. Man we gotta dump her body in an alley. She's an addict so she gonna fit right in."

"Mark this is fucked up." Denise said crying hysterically.

"No, what's fucked up is y'all fucking my night and my money up. We gonna put her in the car and drive around to Lake Merritt. Now let's go. And shut the fuck up!" Mark yelled.

They drove Arlene to an alley in Lake Merritt. It was dark so they could get in and out without drawing too much attention. Denise was crying but was scared of Mark so she cried mostly to herself. Even though they were both addicts, Denise loved Arlene like a sister. Denise thought about all the stories Arlene told her of when she was younger. How happy she was when her oldest child Yvonne was born. How she met and fell in love with Marvin. How she wanted to get clean after Leonard was born. How many times she went to rehab to get cleaned up. How she really loved her family but could never leave the poison alone. Denise thought about who would find Arlene. She thought about how her family was doing in LA. She thought about calling the cops on Mark. Denise felt human again for the first time in many years.

Arlene's body was wrapped in an old carpet from the dope house. Mark placed her body in between some bulk garbage that was out for next day pick up. It didn't matter to him. He was hoping that the garbage men would dump the carpet and not notice the dead body. The entire time, Denise cried and yelled at Mark for making her do this. Denise was in shock and the drugs were leaving her body and she was sobering up real quick. Mark gave Denise an open hand slap to the face. He slapped her so hard it left an imprint on her cheek.

"Bitch if you tell the cops or anyone what happened I fucking kill you and dump you in the Pacific! Got it?"

"Got it." Denise cried in total pain.

Mark dropped Denise off and threatened her again. Denise shook her head in agreement. Denise watched Mark pull off and then headed to the bar on 73rd street. Marvin was at the bar with a beer and Gin & Tonic. Marvin saw when Denise came in. He knew who she was and what she was about. Marvin was drunk like mostly every night. Marvin thought that Arlene was outside so he looked away from Denise. He didn't want to see Arlene tonight. She hadn't been home in a few days and the last time she was she stole money from him. Marvin wanted to kill her but somewhere in his heart he still loved her. He still thought about the love from the 60's. 1988 was on the calendar but his heart and mind said 1968. Marvin at times wished he never had that card game and invited Joey and Mia over. That night ruined Marvin's life and he thought about it every day.

"Marvin, I really need to talk to you." Denise said quietly.

"I ain't got shit to say to you and tell Arlene don't bring her ass home tonight or for the rest of the week. In fact I'm gonna pack her shit and she can move into one of those dope houses." Marvin said in anger.

"Marvin you have to listen to me. Arlene is dead!" Denise shouted.

"Huh?"

"Yeah she passed out tonight and never woke up. She shot up some raw shit and it took her out. I tried to wake her up but she's gone. I want to show you where she is so you can get her and take her somewhere." Denise said covertly.

Marvin knew that this day might one day come. He told himself that he would be prepared. But you can never fully prepare for the death of the only woman you've ever loved. Marvin sat frozen on the bar stool. His eyes were glazed with tears. He couldn't believe what Denise told him. He heard it but he wasn't ready to receive it. He picked up his gin and tonic and downed it like he was a young college fraternity kid racing shots of liquor. Marvin didn't know what to do. He wanted Denise to go back out the door and bring Arlene in. He wanted Denise to say that Arlene was outside and wanted to talk to him. He wished that Arlene was ready to travel over the Bay Bridge to San Francisco and check into the rehab clinic. He wanted to escape from 1988 and go back to playing cards and listening to Motown. He wanted to tuck Alicia and Yvonne in their beds. He wanted to drive to his sister Rosalyn's house in Hayward. Marvin wanted to be anywhere but in East Oakland dealing with the death of his wife.

Chapter 13
Gone,

"*So, you're a philosopher?
Yes, yes, yes, yes, yes
I think very deeply, I think very deeply, I think very deeply*

I think, I think, I think very deeply, I think, I think very deeply

Let's begin, what, where, why, or when Will all be explained like instructions to a game See I'm not insane, in fact, I'm kind of rational When I be asking you, "Who is more dramatical?

"This one or that one, the white one or the black one Pick the punk, and I'll jump up to attack one KRS-One is just the guy to lead a crew Right up to your face and dis you

Everyone saw me on the last album cover Holding a pistol something far from a lover Beside my brother, S C O T T I just laughed, 'cause no one can defeat me This is lecture number two, 'My Philosophy' Number one, was 'Poetry' you know it's me This is my philosophy, many artists got to learn I'm not flammable, I don't burn

"Man this is the shit; yo pass that joint. BDP's new shit is rocking. KRS1 be kicking that shit. This is my favorite new tune. I might play this shit like 10 times in a row. Man ain't nobody fucking with this joint. I really fuck with BDP. The beats be knocking! I wonder what them niggas in New York think about Too Short? I saw his video on YO MTV Raps. Most of the rappers are from the East Coast so when I saw Short I was hype. You know what? I think they fuck with Short. Short got that shit that everybody like. Man he talking about fucking bitches and that's what all niggas like, no matter what coast you on." Leonard was hype. Rewind that shit!"

Leonard was impervious to what happened the night before. He spent the night over one his girlfriend's crib. Little did he know the woman that gave him life died and was dumped in the alley like a piece of garbage. Leonard just got out of juvenile lockup and was catching up on what he missed on the streets. The streets meant more to him than anything that was going on in his house. The juvenile detention center was almost like a second home to Leonard. Leonard had been there off and on the past 6 years. His stays at the detention center began at the age of 12. The staff there knew him very well. They all liked him and thought that if he had a stable home life, he might have a bright future. Leonard never paid much attention to the staff members. He focused on maintaining his respect and doing his time so he could get out and get back to his crew. The crew and his sisters were the only people he cared about. The girls he messed with were just something to do in order to fulfill any sexual desires he had.

Alicia and Yvonne s loved Leonard. They tried to give him all the love and attention that their mom didn't. Leonard loved his sisters and would do anything for them. Sibling love is good but it doesn't equate to the love that a kid desires from his parents. Parental love and care are what kids need. When that is lacking then all hell breaks loose within a kid. Kids that are lacking in that area have the potential to grow up to be predatory teens. Leonard was exactly that. The odds were stacked against Leonard from the time Arlene gave birth to him. Leonard missed the nurturing that a mom provides. Leonard missed the pre-natal care and the love that is necessary when being developed in the womb. Here Leonard was back out of lock up and had no idea the woman he wanted so bad to love and to love him, was dead. Leonard never knew if he could have a real relationship with his mom but he longed for it.

In the depths of her soul Arlene loved Leonard. He was her baby boy. From the time Leonard was born, Arlene knew that he would be special. His brown eyes always mesmerized her when he was a baby. He would cry for her attention and the tears would flow and Arlene would be enveloped by the desire to be needed. Even though Leonard was produced in an environment of drugs and alcohol the love for him was present if only for a short time, Arlene just couldn't keep it up. Many nights Arlene would cry because she knew she wanted to give her children more. She cried because she was an addict and couldn't stay clean. Leonard was her motivation to stay clean during the first two years of his life but then those old demons took over her life. Leonard was always her favorite because he was the only boy. She would always tell anyone who would listen how great Leonard would be one day. Arlene wanted Leonard to represent everything her and Marvin *didn't. She wanted Leonard to make it in spite of her. By the time Leonard was in 1st grade Arlene was at the point of no return. She was so hooked on heroin that she would go days without seeing her children. Leonard would wait up until he passed out from exhaustion waiting for Arlene to come home. Marvin would tell Leonard that his mom was working overtime. When she came home Marvin would clean her up so she would be presentable for Leonard. She might stay home for a few days and then she'd be gone again. That was the pattern during Leonard's entire childhood. Now she was dead and all of the rage Leonard held in would soon be unleashed.*

"Man what are we getting into tonight?" Leonard asked.

"Not sure. Wanna go down Hayward?"

"Nah, whatever we do I want to stay in the in Oaktown; there's gotta be a party popping around Lake Merritt. Call that chick Lisa. She always knows of a good time."

"I'll call her in a few. Hey L did you hit that?"

"Of course I did. I wasn't supposed to say shit, so don't say shit ya dig?"

"Ya secret is safe with me. Maybe her girl Simone will let me tap that. Simone is fine and I know she thinks I'm cute."

"Did she tell you that?" Asked Leonard.

"Nah but you know I can tell."

"Ok. Well dig this call Lisa and see what they are doing." Demanded Leonard.

Leonard and his boys were on the Ave like any other Friday night but this one would be different. Marvin rolled up where Leonard was hanging. Leonard treated his Father different then he treated his mother. Leonard was verbally hard on his father. Marvin tried to be a good man but alcohol and Arlene's drug habit reduced him to a shell of himself. Even though he was the Father and still physically bigger than Leonard, Marvin was intimidated by his son and often times when Marvin was drunk Leonard would talk down to him. Marvin knew that everything Leonard said to him was true but he didn't have the discipline to make a life change. Now Marvin had to summon the strength to tell his only son that his mother was dead.

"Leonard, I really need to talk to you." Marvin uttered.

"Pop's at least you're sober. I just got out of juve the other day. What's up?" Leonard said sarcastically.

'Let's take a walk." Marvin requested.

"Pop, what's going on? You look real fucked up but you ain't drunk. What gives?"

"Leonard, there's no easy way to say this. But something tragic happened last night. Your mother OD'd. She was in the house on Eastmont, kicked it, and somebody dumped her in an alley over in Lake Merritt."

Leonard was silent. The depth of what his father said hadn't fully hit him yet. He knew this day would come, he just didn't know when. Leonard had a blank stare and inside he felt like he got hit with a gut punch. Leonard was a tough teenager. He had dealt with a lot of stress in his young life but this was different. Although his mom had been dead to him, now he would never see her again. There would be no chance to tell her anything. No chance to be a son. No chance to have a real mother. No chance to see what might've been.

"Leonard did you hear me?" Marvin questioned Leonard timidly.

"Yeah man I heard you. Did you tell Alicia and Yvonne?"

"Not yet, I told you first."

"I'll tell them. It's only right since we raised ourselves. Anything else?" Leonard said snippily.

"I have to set up funeral plans and tell Mom's parents. Even though her family cut her off and they blame me for her drug use, I still have to tell them. I don't know what to say to them but I'll have to find a way. "

"Alright I have to get back to the grind." Leonard rushed off.

And with that Leonard was back on the corner with his crew trying to act as normal was possible.

"Hey L your Pop cool? He usually don't roll up on the ave like that."

"Let's hit Churches up and I'll school you on what's going on. My pop just told me that my mom died last night. She was in the dope house up the street in Eastmont and OD'd. Dude dumped her in an alley over at the Lake."

"Damn man. That's fucked up! Man you cool?"

"What can I say? It was bound to happen. She been banging in those arms for years. Them veins can't hold that dope forever. Shit she was like any fiend we gonna serve out here tonight. Only difference is she was my mom."

"The game is fucked up L. That dope don't care who it hit. Shit is like a drive by."

"I know. Hey imma break out and try and reach my sisters. I'll check y'all out tomorrow."

Leonard knew that his dad wasn't going to be home. He probably went to the bar and might end up passing out somewhere. Leonard walked home with a heavy heart. No one could know the pain he was in. At 17 years old he was still a teenager and processed his emotions like a teenager. What he really was, was a boy inside who yearned for a firm family structure. All of those yearnings were now gone forever. Leonard went to his room and kept all of the lights off. He lay on his bed and his mind was racing. He couldn't believe what his pop told him. In shock is what he was. His bedroom felt like a cave with no way out. Visions of a tunnel with boulders blocking the exit flashed in his mind. Taking an axe and smashing the boulder is all he wanted to do. Watching the boulders split in pieces would bring relief to his burdened mind.

Leonard turned on his radio and listened to some hip-hop to try and change his focus. He was having trouble figuring out why he even cared about Arlene. She clearly cared more about heroin then she did her own kids. Leonard wanted his brain to say "fuck her." He rationalized to himself that she deserved what she got for being a drug addict. But deep down Leonard was sad and he really needed a way to express his frustration. That method now was sitting in the dark and blasting some NWA and Boogie Down Productions. Leonard was upset, frustrated, and pissed off; he was pissed off at his parents for being so fucked up. He was mad at himself for being so fucked up. He was mad that his sisters had their shit together but he couldn't stay off the streets. Why couldn't his mom kick the habit? Why did his father allow this to happen?

Why didn't Marvin kill Joey for giving Arlene the heroin at the card game? Why didn't Arlene love him the way she loved the drugs? These were all questions that swirled around in Leonard's brain. Leonard couldn't shake off all of the questions that danced in his head and this long night wouldn't bring any sense of closure.

The darkness and questions remained for hours. Leonard didn't get any sleep. He sat in the dark all night listening to music and thinking about Arlene. He wasn't sure what to do next. Was he going to go to the funeral? When was the funeral? Would he ever speak to his father again? When would he call his sisters? When would he be able to sleep? His brain and heart were in sync and racing faster than ever. Would he continue to hustle on the streets? What the fuck was he going to do with his life?

Before this night Leonard never thought about his future. He never had a world view and never saw past Oakland. Because his mind was all over the place, he now began to think about things he never thought of before. He would be 18 in a few months and a legit adult. He might be back at juvenile detention because of a fight he had with some dude from San Fran. Fucking around on the BART got him in trouble. He was used to the detention center but after 18 he would be eligible for state prison. Prison seemed like it was inevitable for everybody in his crew. They looked at it as a rite of passage.

It was now 6am and Leonard had been up all night. His eyes were still full of tears. The 17- year old man of the streets had been reduced to an elementary kid on the inside. Emotionally he was in the 4th grade; which was the last time he can remember having any level of family normalcy. He prepared to call both of his sisters. First he would call Yvonne and then Alicia. Yvonne was in college and Leonard had the number to her dorm room.

"Hello."

"He Yvonne, its Leonard."

"Hey baby bro. What's up?"

"Mom was found dead in an alley last night. She OD'd in a dope house in Eastmont and they dumped her body in Lake Merritt. Pop stopped by the Ave and told me last night. I haven't seen him since. Not sure about any funeral arrangements. Can you call Alicia? I don't really feel like talking right now. "

"I knew this day would happen, I just didn't know when. I had a feeling when I heard your voice that something happened. I'm going to have to come home and help Pop with the funeral arrangements. I'm sad but she's been dead since we were kids. Leonard I know she loved us but she was a stone cold drug addict. She's the reason why I don't drink or party at all. I don't want to end up like her. There are going to be a lot of people stopping by the house so you might want to lay low for a few days. It's up to you. I'll be home later this afternoon. Thanks for letting me know Leonard. I'll see you later and I want a big hug from you!"

Leonard hung up with his sister and headed out the door. Leonard couldn't stay at the house anymore. He needed to be with his crew and he didn't want to see any of his family members. He knew his pop would be putting on a show for the people who stopped by. Marvin had been at the bar damn near the whole time since he told Leonard about Arlene's death. Just like his early childhood, Alicia and Yvonne would be doing the motherly duties. They were the only motherly figures that he had and he looked forward to seeing them. He needed companionship and comfort from his older sisters. That would come later but for now he would be back with the crew and who knows how that would turn out.

Chapter 14
The last Straw

Leonard had been on the Ave since noon. It was now after 9 pm and he went through all the emotions of the night before. He masked a lot of it through smoking weed and drinking 40's of Ole E. Unlike his sisters, Leonard didn't stay away from alcohol. He knew how it fucked his Pop's life up but he always rationalized that he wouldn't end up like that because he didn't drink hard liquor. The crew was up no good as usual and Leonard was really fucked up. He had trouble getting his thoughts clear. He was seeing double and had some dark thoughts about hurting someone. He was eyeballing his crew thinking of someone to start an argument with but they showed him so much love all day, he couldn't do it. The thoughts only intensified the more he drank.

"T, I'm breaking out. Going to In N Out and getting a burger."

"You headed to the coliseum?"

"Yeah."

"I'll roll with you. I need something to eat and the block is hot right now."

"Let's take the bus over there. Maybe we can meet some dips while we're on it."

"Let's go."

People got on and off the bus. It was only a few stops between Eastmont and the coliseum, maybe 10 minutes. It seemed like forever to Leonard. His head was spinning and he still felt like he needed to hurt someone. Somebody had to pay for Arlene and Marvin being so fucked up. Somebody had to pay for all the trips he had to the juvenile detention center. Somebody had to pay for him not having shit. It didn't matter who paid, as long as it was someone. By this point in the night nothing mattered; not his sisters coming home, the funeral, helping his pop, none of it mattered. The only thing that mattered was retribution. Society owed Leonard Smith a debt and society was going to pay tonight. Polo, an associate of the Ave Crew got one at the stop right after Eastmont. Polo was a lot like Leonard. He was a ruthless teenager that was street-wise way beyond his years. He respected Leonard and the whole crew. And he was locked with Leonard at Juve. Sometimes he hung with them on Bancroft. Polo was a born hustler and gambler. His father got shot at a card game back in the 70's. Polo had a fuck it attitude and Polo was only loyal to himself.

"Ave crew. What's up gang? Where y'all headed?"

"To the coliseum to get a bite to eat. Where you going?"

"I was going over to the city, but now I'll roll with y'all if that's cool."

"Yeah man I'm good with that."

T did most of the talking to Polo. Leonard was quiet and staring straight ahead. He knew that his life was soon about to change. Coliseum stop was next. Leonard saw an older lady (Patty Hayes) get on the bus. Leonard watched her get on the bus and stalked her like a Lion in the jungles of Africa. She was now prey for Leonard. Patty bared a strong resemblance to Arlene and that made Leonard angrier than he already was. Leonard told himself that she was it. This stranger, whom he never saw before tonight, had to pay for everything he hated about his 17 years of existence. He watched her sit down and put her purse on her lap. Patty pulled an Ebony Magazine out of her purse and began to flip through the pages. Leonard's face was filled with rage. The alcohol and pain had taken over his mind. At this point he no ability to exhibit rational thoughts. Patty didn't pay any attention to the Ave Crew. She was engrossed in the magazine and was listening to Michael Jackson on her Walkman. Leonard eyed her the whole time.

The Coliseum stop was next. When the bus stops you have to go up a dark stairwell to get to the area where the stores are. T, Polo, and Leonard were ready to get off, as was Patty. The bus came to a stop and all 4 individuals got off. Patty was in front, still with her Walkman on. The 3 teenagers followed behind with T and Polo talking about what they were going to get to eat. Leonard knew that the steps would be the best place to make his move. He didn't want to tell the other two because they may try and talk him out of it. Polo and T continued to talk. Leonard watched Patty intensely and as she took her next step, he leaped into action.

Leonard hit her with a closed fist in the side of the face. Patty's Walkman flew off of her head and slammed into the concrete. Patty was stunned and immediately hit the ground. She was bleeding out of her mouth and nose. Leonard began to kick her in her ribs. Patty screamed for T and Polo to help her. Polo and T stood in shock. They didn't know what happened and weren't sure if they should intervene. Leonard started yelling at Patty.

"You look like the bitch that ruined my life. I wish she died years ago. Now I want you to die. You feel the pain. You feel what it's like to not be able to breathe."

"Who are you and why are you doing this"? Patty screamed to Leonard.

"Shut the fuck up you dumb bitch." Leonard kicked her again and then slapped her in the face. T began to intervene. T could see above the stairs to the platform. He saw two BART police officers walking on the platform. T knew that they would hear Patty screaming and they would get caught in Leonard's bullshit. T grabbed Leonard by the arm and pulled him away from Patty. Patty was on the ground writhing in pain. She was crying and started to scream at the top of her lungs.
"HELP ME. Somebody please help me!"

"Yo, BART cops are right up on the platform. We gotta get the fuck out of here. L c'mon man we gonna get popped."

Polo watched in horror. He couldn't believe what he was seeing. He was hardcore dude and would fuck a nigga up quick but this was some other shit. Polo didn't advocate hitting a woman. He loved his sisters and his aunts. He was amazed at what Leonard was doing to this stranger. For a moment Polo wanted to kill Leonard. Polo wanted to help Patty but knew that he might get jumped if he tried to help her. Leonard and Todd were like blood brothers and Polo knew this. Polo's mind was racing. Just like Leonard he was on probation and didn't want to go back to the detention center. Polo was stuck on the stairs in this madness and ready to kill Leonard.

"Yo let's go."

"What about her? Man we can't leave her here like this."

"Listen those cops are right up on the platform. The next time she opens her mouth they're going to hear her. We have to break out right now, if not we're all in shit. These BART cops shoot first and ask questions later. They'll find her. She won't die. But we're outta here."

"HELP ME, please HELP ME! Patty screamed again!

Patty was now screeching in horror at the top of her lungs and this time the BART cops heard her. The boys could hear the keys jingling and the BART patrol on the radio calling for back up. They were hurrying fast towards Patty and intensity was in their faces. Patty was hurt but she was a fighter. She screamed again because she also heard the BART cops approaching. She had hope in her eyes. Leonard wanted to kick her again but now he knew it was time to break out. This scene was bloody and trouble was in the air. T and Polo were ready to leave Leonard.

The cops hit the top step and headed towards the scene. The three boys took off and 3 BART officers made chase. By the time they hit the stairs, back up had arrived and the one officer stayed with Patty until EMT arrived. The BART cops ordered the 3 teens to stop running and give up. That wasn't going to happen and the boys were too far for the cops to shoot at them. All three were in stride together. As they were running they told each other to head to International Blvd. It was probably a mile on foot but the adrenaline was pumping and they had to get away. It was blacktop so it seemed like smooth sailing getting away from the cops. They could take a couple of shortcuts off of the BLVD and head to a safe house. But first they had to elude the cops. The cops were giving an intense chase and giving them orders to surrender the entire time.

They were almost off of the coliseum parking lot when Polo tripped and fell. T and Leonard looked back and saw him falling. They knew they couldn't stop and help and yelled back to him to get up and c'mon. But the cops were closing in fast and pulled their guns out as they approached Polo on the ground.

Leonard never stopped running towards the safe house. Todd was right in step and the whole time he was thinking how the hell he got into this situation. He thought they were going to In N Out and then over to the lake to hang with some girls.

"Freeze mother fucker! Hands let me see your hands. Hands on the ground palms down. You make a move and I'll blow your brains out."

"Don't shoot my hands are right here." Polo pleaded.

"Hands behind your back."

The BART police now had Polo in custody. Polo's mind, like Todd's, was spinning. He had no idea how he was now handcuffed and waiting for the Oakland Police Department. He was thinking to himself, "Who the fuck was that chick and what the fuck was Leonard thinking?" He also knew not to make a move around the Oakland PD. They shoot young niggas for sport with no fear of consequences. He would have to figure out what the charges were and go from there. Polo had been in trouble enough times to know how to manipulate the system. The problem he had now was the fact that he was on probation and this shit with Patty had nothing to do with him. He sat there waiting for Oakland PD and was mad at himself that he didn't roll out as soon as Leonard punched that chick. BART cops asked him who he was and why "they" beat Patty up. Polo didn't want to talk to BART cops because he thought that they would lie to Oakland PD. He told them he wasn't talking to them. He would call a public defender when he got to the station house. He was still a minor and technically didn't have to say anything without a parent present. That wouldn't happen for him because he had no way to contact his mother. He might be able to call his grandmother but he wasn't sure.

Oakland PD showed up and they wanted blood. BART cops told the OPD what happened to Patty on the steps. OPD knew that there were three perpetrators and that 2 of them fled on foot into the darkness. OPD for now focused all of their attention on Polo. Polo was a tough street kid but sitting there on the concrete in the dark, he was now scared of the OPD. A woman beaten up in the BART station was not a good look. OPD had no love for young black teenagers in Oakland. Here sat a hard working tax paying woman beaten up in a BART station. BART took pride in making sure their stations were safe for everyone. A lot of white Oakland residents used BART to get around the Bay area and a high percentage of them worked in San Francisco. BART made sure that safety was paramount to their daily operations. OPD was aware of the BART's attempts to be proactive when it came to crime. That's why they were always very vigilant at BART stations. The coliseum BART station was very busy and the neighborhood was seedy which led to increased patrols but that BART station had violence around the perimeter.

OPD snatched Polo off the ground and slammed his head on the car hood.

"Where's the other two?"

"I don't know." Screamed Polo.

"Not good enough." OPD slammed Polo's head on the hood once again.

"I'm gonna ask you again, where are your boys?"

"Told you I don't know."

"Ok. So you're a wiseass. How about I put this club upside you're head? Think that will jog your memory?"

"I'm telling you I don't know anything."

"Alright so that's how it's going to be. Brad, Let's take him to the station and book him."

Polo sat in the interrogation room at the Oakland Police Traffic Division. The room was cramped and smelled like cigarettes and old cologne. A dim light hung from the ceiling and the paint was chipping on the walls. The floor was concrete and the table was missing a leg. You could tell that many murder interrogations had taken place in this room. Polo had a cup of water and a candy bar in front of him. Polo had been arrested before but he knew this was different. Leonard damn near killed that chick. Polo still couldn't understand what the fuck Leonard was thinking. Right now Polo was thinking about what the cops would ask him and what he would say. Damn he was in a tight spot. He was already on probation and one fuck up could get him locked up in juve until he was 21. That's a bid he didn't want to do. "Fuck fuck fuck" is what Polo said to himself as he saw detective Ellis through the glass in the door.

Detective Solomon Ellis was an old school detective. He was an intimidating figure. He stood 6'4" 260lbs. His hair and beard were both salt & pepper. He fancied a toothpick every day and drank 3 cups of coffee daily. He was one of the first black detectives in Oakland. He had been on the force for almost 40 years. He could've retired two years ago but this is all he knew. His wife of 40 years wanted him home and he promised her that by the end of '89 he would be retiring. He wore a double-breasted suit to work every day and a Fedora. Detective Smith knew that most of the teenagers that got arrested would sing like a bird once they got popped. They didn't want to do adult prison time and therefore would cut a deal and stay in juvenile detention center. He figured he would do the same with Polo. Ellis entered the room with a file in his hand and a toothpick in his mouth.

"I'm detective Ellis. I've seen all of you young punks throughout my 40 years on the force. Don't bullshit me at all. I'll make your life real tough and also make sure that the judge roofs your ass with the time. That being said, you're going to tell me everything I want to know. Understand?" Polo shook his head in agreement.

"So Mr. Lowe (Desmond Lowe was Polo's real name) I'd like for you to take a look at these." Detective Smith showed Polo pictures of Patty and her beaten face.

"Patty Hayes is a single mom living in East Oakland. She was coming from work in San Leandro. Do you have a job? No didn't think so. This woman is hard working and trying to have a better life for her and her children. And you and your friends decide to attack her for nothing. You young punks didn't even rob her. So why would three young thugs attack a stranger? Did she say something to you guys? I'm pretty sure y'all were drinking and smoking all night. Patty told my guys she's never seen any of you. So I'm wondering what's going on here? Well I'll tell you like this Desmond. If I don't hear what I want I'm going to charge you with attempted murder. You'll be someone's bitch for the next 20 years. I have to take a piss. I'll leave you this file and give you time to think about San Quentin. When I come back in this room you got one chance to tell me what I want to hear. Dig it?"

Polo was fucked and he knew it. If he snitched on Leonard and Todd then he would be a marked man on the streets. His name would be mud and he would lose all street credibility and his life would be on the line. If he stayed true to the code of the streets, which means no snitching to the cops, then he was looking at adult prison time for some shit that he had nothing to do with. This was a crazy situation for him to be in. He knew that detective Ellis wouldn't let him make a phone call or honor any of his other civil rights. With his rap sheet Polo was lucky he wasn't already in juve. Polo knew that Ellis wanted to know who Todd and Leonard were and where he could find them. Polo didn't know what to do but he had to come up with something quick. Ellis was still out on his bathroom break.

This stall game is what the cops do when they think they can break somebody. Polo was hip to the game; he figured Ellis would give him a few more minutes and then come in with the plea deal. Polo stared at the wall racking his brain on what to do. He had to deal with this old school detective in a matter of minutes. Polo took a sip of water and made up his mind on how he was going to handle the situation.

"Hey Ellis I just got this in. One of the BART cops picked this up near the victim."

"Good. Tell those BART guys we'll take them over to the city for dinner and drinks."

The BART cops found Leonard's juvenile detention center ID card. It must've fell out of his hoodie pocket when he was assaulting Patty. It still had blood on it. Smith ran his name through the system and it came back with a long rap sheet. Multiple arrests showed for Leonard and the fact that he was on probation meant Ellis now had everything he needed. Ellis never heard of Smith before.

"Hey Brad have you ever heard of this kid? His sheet is long and he has some violent priors on here. Charles just gave this piece of evidence from the scene. He said the BART guys found it. I ran him through and this is what came back."

"Yeah he runs with some young boys over there on Bancroft. And I know his grandfather Cecil. Good man but left for

San Diego years ago and rarely comes back to visit. Smith is a product of the streets. Word is he's nobody to fuck with."

"Why would he want to assault this hard working woman? She doesn't seem like the type to mess with his crowd. Something's not adding up. I'm going to talk to this other creep we have in the box. I'm going to scare his ass but I know he didn't have anything to do with this so I'll let him walk but he'll sit for a few more minutes."

Ellis walked back into the box with Leonard's ID in a plastic bag. Ellis took his jacket off so Polo could see the gun sticking off of his side in the holster.

"Hey Polo. Yeah I ran your name and got your rap sheet. You're already on probation so that means if we get a conviction, and we will, you're skinny black ass will be headed to San Quentin. So you ready to tell me what I want to hear? You give me a name and location and you can walk out of here free and clear."

"Man I didn't touch that woman."

"That's not what I want to hear."

"I was headed to the coliseum by myself to get something to eat. I knew those dudes from the streets and juve and they said they were getting something eat too. When we got off the BART dude just snapped. I looked back and he was kicking that lady on the ground. I never saw her before. I didn't know what to do. Listen, I was ready to kill him. He was in total violation of the street code. Man, we never hit women. I can't go down for this bullshit."

"Well son it's good to know that you value something in your life. "

Detective Ellis showed Polo the plastic bag with the ID in it. Polo was shook up. He saw the blood on the ID and got mad again. Polo lost respect for Leonard on that stairwell and was ready to deal with the blowback. In Polo's mind he was mad enough to kill Leonard so if he snitched it didn't bother him. Fuck Leonard is what Polo told himself!

"So here it is Desmond, I have Leonard's name and address but I know he won't be staying there tonight. So all I need you to do is tell me where I can grab him tomorrow and what time."

"He'll be at 75th and Olive tomorrow around Noon. It's the routine for those cats."

"Desmond, I appreciate your help. I won't mention this to Leonard. I'm going to show him the ID so you'll be in the clear. Now you need to keep your ass in check. I know who you are and I'll be on your ass if I get a chance. You gave me a play here so I'll give you a break but this is the only one. Hear me?"

"I got you. Can I roll out? I'm still hungry."

"Yeah go get something to eat and keep your ass out of trouble!"

Ellis rubbed his face with his heart pounding. He wanted to make sure Leonard was locked under the jail. San Quentin wasn't enough for him. Ellis wanted him to go to Patton State. He knew that would give Leonard the ass whipping he deserved. Ellis was tired of seeing these young black teenagers in the precinct on a nightly basis. The cat and mouse game kept Solomon young but he knew he couldn't keep doing this. He was now on a mission to get Leonard Smith. His plan was to have backup and grab him tomorrow afternoon. He figured Leonard would never suspect Polo of snitching or dropping his ID, so he would be out there on 75th tomorrow. Right now Ellis was ready to go home hug his wife and get some sleep. First thing in the morning he would visit Patty and then grab this young punk!

Chapter 15
Cuffed,

It was high Noon the next day and like clockwork Leonard and the boys were out on 75th and Olive. Leonard had no idea that Detective Smith was on his ass. Leonard had a major hangover from the night before. He stopped at Church's chicken and got a 4pc with biscuit, fries and a large Coke. He ate that shit within a few minutes. His body needed the grease to soak up the alcohol. He still had a headache but his teenage body was able to bounce back very quickly. Leonard didn't remember a lot about the night before. He vaguely remembered hitting a woman at the BART but didn't know exactly why? He also couldn't figure out why his boots had dry blood on them. He figured maybe he stepped in some blood when he was running from the BART last night. He sat still for 5 minutes trying to think of everything that happened last night. It started to come back to him in bits and pieces. He looked down at the blood and figured he would go take his boots off and put on some sneakers.

"Yo L man what the fuck? Cuz you were tripping last night! Man that was some crazy shit. You know I'm with you and we tight but that was some other shit. Nigga you snapped the fuck out. I hope that shit don't come back to bite us. Those BART cops were on our ass and Polo tripped and got popped by OPD. Me & Polo had no idea what the fuck was going on."

"I almost forgot Polo tripped and got popped. Damn man my bad."

"What did that chick do to you?" Todd chuckled, "You hit that bitch like she was Marco."

Leonard laughed and said "she looked like him a little bit."

"Yeah she did."

"Man I had a pounding headache this morning. I might have to cool out from the 40's tonight. We need to forget about last night and head over to the Lake tonight and get with those slimmies."

"Yeah you're right about that, nigga you need some pussy."

"Yeah I do."

"When is the funeral for your Mom?"

"Not sure I have to talk to my sister Yvonne later. I ain't even sure I'm going. Ain't like she was a real mom to us. She was out here in the streets."

"I hear that. Hey man I'm hungry, I'm ready to go to Church's and get a 4pc."

"I just got one. You go ahead I'll chill here and keep my eye on the stash. These cats fucked up the count yesterday and we need some money to get these bitches later."

"Alright I'll be back."

The Ave crew was hustling some dope in East Oakland so Leonard had to be out there and make sure everything was cool. There were some older cats in the crew but they couldn't beat Leonard so he ran shit. Everyone was still young and spent the money on bitches, beer and food. Todd wanted to buy a car next week. He had been saving money to buy one. Leonard's probation officer advised him not to get one because he would make sure he got caught underage drinking and driving. Leonard was going to be on probation until 21. He figured fuck it, he would wait until then to buy a car and until then he would ride with Todd.

The sun was shining in East Oakland and the crew was out there working and fucking around like teenagers do. A couple of dudes were slap boxing, two others were racing pole to pole, another was telling how he fucked some bitch from LA last night and Leonard was watching them and the whole time he was still in pain from Arlene's death. These guys didn't know how much pain Leonard was in. All they knew is that his mom died but he didn't fuck with her anyway so it didn't matter. Nor did they know what happened last night at the Coliseum BART, but they would soon find out.

Todd was still at Church's eating. Leonard thought about checking on Polo but he didn't want to sniff around OPD. He knew

Polo wasn't a snitch dude and could take whatever the police threw at him. If Polo had to go back to Juve Leonard would take care of him on the money tip. Leonard didn't want to think that far ahead. As soon as Todd came to the corner he was going to go home and take a nap. He felt like he hadn't slept in days. Yvonne said she was going to make dinner later. Leonard planned to sleep all day, eat dinner with his sisters and then head over to the Lake with Todd. His plan was in place he just needed Todd to hit the corner and he was gone.

Detective Ellis had two unmarked cars along with the OPD SWAT team parked around the corner. He was a block away and could see the Ave crew on the corner of 75th and Olive. They were going to move in when he gave the word. Ellis made sure he had a couple of young SWAT members with him to make the arrest. They would treat Leonard like the criminal he was. They weren't taking any unnecessary risks with him or his crew. OPD SWAT was known for shooting first and asking questions later. They were in position in the backyard of the house where Leonard was standing. Typically the Ave Crew didn't sell a lot of dope during the day so they never paid attention to their surroundings. Ellis was parked in an' 84 Navy Blue Caprice Classic. He wanted to get Leonard apprehended without SWAT killing him. Ellis wanted to get Leonard in the box, get a whole confession on tape, and give him 20 years in the state prison system.

The SWAT team was on the walkie-talkie with Detective Ellis. Ellis let them know they would be making a move in 60 seconds. There was a civilian in the area and Ellis didn't want to take any chances in case Leonard or one of the crew members had a gun and started firing. Todd came out of Church's Chicken and could see the crew on the corner of 75th. He started to head down the street and he heard a huge voice yell out "Freeze Mother Fucker!!!!!"

"You take a step and I'll blow your fucking head off. On the ground with your hands behind your back. Now!"

Todd stopped in his tracks and saw two plain clothes officers, two SWAT team dudes and he saw detective Ellis walking up the street with his gun out. All of the crew was face down on the ground in a spread position. The biggest SWAT guy had a gun to back the back of Leonard's head. He whispered in Leonard's ear, "give me a reason to put a hole in you pussy." Leonard didn't move and was frozen with fear. Todd ducked behind a tree and looked behind him to make sure no one was going to put a gun to his head.

Ellis put his gun away and strolled on the scene. His toothpick was in his mouth and he was ready to put Leonard away. Ellis surveyed the area and gave a nod to the SWAT to back off. Ellis wanted to put the cuffs on Leonard himself. SWAT still had the gun pointed at him. Ellis made sure the other members searched the crew for drugs and weapons. He called for the OPD van to come around and all of the crew were handcuffed and loaded in the Van. Ellis would check names and see if any of them were on probation or had warrants; if so, they were getting locked up today with Leonard. Leonard was still on the ground.

"On your feet Smith and keep your hands where I can see them. You make a move and this dude will put a bullet in your ass that the doctors can't fix. Pat him down and make sure he's clean. If he has a gun on him maybe we'll shoot him and say it was self-defense." Leonard was now scared to death. He had no idea why he was being arrested? He was still trying to sober up and clear his head. He knew if he tried to run that the big white SWAT dude would definitely shoot him. He figured that this old black guy wasn't going to be much help. Leonard figured he was detective because of the suit. Why are they fucking with us?" Leonard thought to himself. Detectives only come around when there's a homicide. The crew was hustling and robbing but they hadn't killed anyone. Leonard didn't want to get killed so he followed all instructions from detective Ellis.

"He's clean Ellis."

"Smith you under arrest for aggravated assault and attempted murder. You have the right to remain silent. You have the right to an attorney." Ellis read Leonard all of his Miranda rights.

"Do you understand?"

"Leonard nodded in agreement."

"No mother fucker answer yes or no."

"Yes."

"Turn your bitch ass around. These are my special cuffs so I'll make sure they're extra tight. In fact, cuff his ankles too. This bitch might get the feeling to run off."

Leonard was cuffed wrists and ankles and placed in the back of Ellis's car. Ellis had his partner with him and just to fuck with Leonard. They made sure they talked about teenagers getting raped in prison. Leonard had heard it all before but now it felt real to him. He knew that this ride was different. He also knew that this was about the shit that happened last night. He tried to figure how they knew he did it. No way Polo snitched, he thought, Polo wasn't that type of dude plus Polo knew that Leonard would kill him. The ride to the precinct would be the longest of his life.

Todd watched the whole thing go down and was scared to death. Todd knew that this was all about that incident last night at the Coliseum. He was cussing Leonard out in head. "Why the fuck did he do that?" That was all Todd could think about. He knew last night that this shit was fucked up and he was in the mix. As Todd watched the car roll down the block he knew he wasn't going to see Leonard for a long time. Todd didn't know what to do. All he knew was that all of his friends were headed to the precinct and he didn't know when he would see them again. Silence had now taken over 75th and Olive Street. Todd looked down the block at the Ave and for the first time in years it was empty.

"Keep him shackled and put him in the box. Don't give him shit until I get in there."

"Ellis you don't fuck around. You said you were going to get him at Noon and you got him. Was it hard?"

"Not at all. Those young punks were right on the same corner that they're on every day and night. I made sure to have those two young Swat guys, James & Bryant. They scared the shit out of those kids. A bunch of them are in the Paddy van. Process them until I get over there. I'm going to deal with this main perp. I'm going to ensure that he gets the maximum time. Before I go in the box I'll call William and see what charges he can make stick.

William Robinson was the District Attorney (D.A) of Alameda County, the county in which the city of Oakland resides. William was firm but fair. He understood the drug epidemic and how it affected kids and their behavior. He would often send kids to residential treatment facilities as opposed to the juvenile detention center. Juvenile detention was reserved for only the violent teenagers. He wasn't going to fill up the detention centers with kids that engage in petty crimes. However the one thing he wouldn't tolerate is violence against hard-working women. The last case he had similar to Leonard's, he made sure that the kid did state time in an adult prison.

"William, good morning."

"Detective Ellis what can I do for you?"

"I had my intern drop a file on your desk this morning. Did you get it?"

"Yeah I got it. I haven't looked at it yet. Hold the phone I'll read it while I got you on the line. Ellis, yeah I've seen his name before. Uh huh, so he assaulted an innocent woman on her way home from work. And I see he's still on probation. One thing I can't tolerate is when these young punks pick on innocent civilians. If they want to fight and kill each other than so be it but assaulting the innocent will not be tolerated. If he pleads guilty he'll get 5-10 years in state prison. If he goes to trial he'll be doing 10-20 and let him know that I'll make sure that all that 20 gets done with no parole. Do you have him at the precinct?"

"Yeah he's here in the box."

"OK, offer him the deal and call me back. We'll work directly on this deal. Usually I'd have Epps work on this but this one is mine. Smith will learn a lesson on this one. His juvenile time is over. He'll be charged as an adult."

"Thanks William I'll call you back after I talk to him."

"No problem."

Ellis hung up and grabbed the file on his desk. It was a manila folder with a few pictures of Patty's bloody face. This was an old school police technique in order to try and get the suspect to dig within and find some humanity. Ellis really didn't care since he had the bloody I.D. and also Polo's testimony if he needed it. The pictures of Patty would hopefully make Smith's process faster. No matter what, Leonard was done. Just hanging with Polo was a violation of his probation. So automatically Leonard was being held. Today was different thought because now he would be doing adult time.

Ellis entered in the box and placed the file in front of Leonard.

"Can I get some water?"

"No mother fucker, when you tell me what I want to hear maybe I'll think about bringing you some water."

"C'mon man just a cup and then we can rap."

"Listen here you little bitch. You ain't getting shit from me and don't hit me with any of your street bullshit. I'm in charge here. You're not on 75th. I'm going to let you look at this file and I'll be back in a few."

Ellis got up and closed the door. He stayed right by the box and peered through at the window and kept his eyes fixed on Leonard. He knew the file trick worked about 95% of the time but there was that 5% of the time when it didn't. Ellis couldn't have imagined what happened next.

Leonard was still shackled wrists and ankles. He could move his hands and slid the pictures even closer. He looked at them for about 30 seconds and started sobbing uncontrollably. Ellis stepped back in amazement. Smith had a reputation for being a tough son of a bitch. Ellis kept on watching. Leonard cried very deeply for 5 straight minutes. He kept apologizing to the pictures and uttered "it wasn't you it was her." Ellis figured he would let him get it out and then go get the information he needed.

Ellis wasn't moved at all by Leonard's tears. Ellis knew what he saw when he visited Patty in the hospital earlier in the morning. Her face is what would move Smith. He would make sure that all interaction with Smith would be done with Patty in mind. After 10 minutes Ellis was ready to go in and put the screws to Leonard. Robinson's office had faxed over the plea deal for Leonard to sign. Ellis put the deal paper and the bloody I.D. in a folder and headed into the box.

"See you mother fuckers are real tough when y'all are beating up on innocent women but now you see the pictures and you want to cry like a bitch. You're crying because you know those pictures mean you crossed over from juvenile detention to the big boys. The cats doing life hate when bitch ass dudes like you hit women. They are yearning for some pussy and here you are-about to give them what they want. Well Smith you did it this time. We can play this two ways. It's up to you how it's going down."

Leonard placed his head in his shirt trying to wipe the tears that were still left. Ellis didn't bother to unshackle him nor offer him a tissue. Leonard wasn't about to get any sympathy from Solomon. Solomon simply wanted to get his signature on that plea deal and send it back to William.

"I'm not even going to ask if you did it. I know you did it so we can skip the bullshit. I checked your file Smith, you are currently on probation until you're 21. That means you can kiss the streets good bye. You won't be seeing them for a while. The next time you see them is up to you. I spoke to District Attorney William Robinson. Mr. Robinson has heard of you before. I guess so since you've been arrested 89 times since the age of 11. Mr. Robinson is done giving you chances to get your shit together. So here's the deal. You have two choices. 1st choice is plead guilty as an adult to aggravated assault and pay victim restitution. That deal is 5-10 years state time. The 2nd choice is go to trial and if convicted, which you will be, the term is 10-20 years and Robinson stated that you would do all 20 years with no chance for parole."

Ellis took the cuffs off of Leonard's wrists. Leonard was still shackled at the ankles and Smith had no intentions of letting him loose.

"I have to hit the head. Here's a pen. By the time I get back I want a signature on whichever deal you accept. It will be less than 5 minutes so think fast."

Leonard sat there pen in his hand knowing that his life as he knew it was over. Why why why was all his brain kept repeating? Why did his parents have to be so fucked up? Why couldn't he get his shit together like his sisters? Why did he hit this woman last night? California adult prisons were nothing like the juvenile detention center in Oakland. They were going to ship his ass out and he might end up at San Quentin, Pelican Bay or Patton. Leonard was a tough guy no more. He was now a seventeen-year old teenager faced with the prospect of doing time with the worst and hardest criminals in California. Tears welled up in his eyes once again. Childhood was over. Hanging with the crew and going to Hayward and over to the Lake was over. The last time Leonard was at the detention center one of the counselors tried to explain to him how rough state prison was, especially for a teenager. Like all the other speeches Leonard received it went in one ear and out of the other. Now that speech was all Leonard could think about. Why didn't he listen to that counselor? Why didn't he take advantage of the wilderness programs that the center offered? Why was the theme of the 5 minutes that detective Ellis was out of the box. Leonard signed the deal so when Ellis came back he could face whatever was going to happen next.

"Pen is down so I guess you signed. Let's see here. Smart man you took the 5-10. Really wasn't an option. No one would want to do that full 20- year term. A skinny punk like you might not even make it 20 years. Shit you might not make it a week before they rape you. If you resist they might kill you after they rape you. Your days in Juve are over. I saw in your file that your Dad had a phone number but since you're being tried as an adult we don't have to call him. I'll call him myself and let him know when you're sentencing date is. Stand up and put your hands behind your back."

Ellis cuffed Leonard one more time and escorted him to the back of precinct. The prison van headed to Santa Rita jail was leaving in a few minutes. That's where Leonard would be until he got sentenced. He already knew how much time he was getting, he just didn't know where. Leonard told himself not to cry anymore. He had to toughen up right now. Once he got in that van he had to man up. He couldn't be a bitch at Santa Rita. He knew a few dudes up there so he might be safe but shit was totally different than the center.

"Patty Hayes."

"Huh?"

"Patty Hayes is the name of the woman you beat up last night. When you get sentenced she'll be in the courtroom. She might persuade the judge or Robinson to make you do the 10 years straight. You better hope she's a nice woman because she can make your life real miserable. I don't see why she wouldn't. You could've killed her if your boys didn't grab you off of her. No matter what I'll be there in the courtroom and the judge will see these pictures. Just remember her name and let that shit keep you up at night. She has 2 kids and works hard. That's something your low-life ass knows nothing about. I'll see you again Smith."

Detective Ellis hit the side door and the officers inside opened it. There were two armed guards inside of the van along with 5 other dudes that were shackled. The guards had shotguns ready to snipe if the criminals got unruly. Ellis instructed the guards not unshackle any of the prisoners under any circumstances. Ellis whispered something to one of the guards and pointed at Leonard, which shook him up. It was a bumpy ride on the way to Santa Rita. The van stunk and there were no windows in the back. The fact that the van was dark was a metaphor for the entirety of Leonard's life. Leonard gazed straight ahead and mouthed out loud, "Patty Hayes why did you get on the bus last night?"

Part 3

Chapter 16
East Oakland,

Some say the blacker the berry, the sweeter the juice I say the darker the flesh then the deeper the roots I give a holler to my sisters on welfare Tupac cares, if don't nobody else care And uhh, I know they like to beat ya down a lot When you come around the block brothas clown a lot But please don't cry, dry your eyes, never let up Forgive but don't forget, girl keep your head up And when he tells you you ain't nothin' don't believe him And if he can't learn to love you you should leave him Cause sista you don't need him And I ain't tryin to gas up, I just call em how I see em You know it makes me unhappy When brothas make babies, and leave a young mother to be a pappy And since we all came from a woman Got our name from a woman and our game from a woman I wonder why we take from our women Why we rape our women, do we hate our women? I think it's time to kill for our women Time to heal our women, be real to our women And if we don't we'll have a race of babies That will hate the ladies, that make the babies And since a man can't make one He has no right to tell a woman when and where to create one So will the real men get up I know you're fed up ladies, but you gotta keep your head up"

That's what Leonard heard blasting through the car speakers as he exited the prison bus at the Oakland Coliseum. Hip-Hop music had changed in the 5 years since he left for PSP. He used to listen to Too Short, NWA, Ice-T, Rakim, PE, Big Daddy Kane, and LL Cool J. He didn't know who was out now. He heard some of the younger dudes at PSP talking about some of the new groups like Wu Tang, Snoop and Biggie, but he didn't pay it much attention at PSP. He was all about boxing and reading. He asked the girl at the bus stop who that was rapping and she let him know it was 2Pac and he lived in Oakland. Leonard shook his head in acknowledgement and knew he heard that name at PSP. He liked the sound and was going to buy the tape as a soon as he got a chance.

Leonard couldn't believe it. He was back in Oaktown. He didn't know what to do. Usually his days in prison were spent in the dungeon and reading in his cell. This was his first day of freedom since '88. At PSP and also from letters his sister wrote, Leonard knew that gang activity had picked up in Oaktown. He would have to navigate the streets the same he did at PSP. Shit was different out here. The survival of the fittest was always the number one rule as was being careful whom you trusted. Leonard hadn't seen any of his old friends since he got sent to PSP. A lot of them also spent time in juvenile lock up and a couple of them were sent to prison down in Southern California. Leonard wanted to get something to eat and walked over to the In N Out burger spot in the coliseum parking lot. He ordered the number 1 animal style with lemonade as his choice of beverage. He only had outside food twice at PSP. He got his food and sat outside of In N Out. He admired the palm trees, the people driving around, the blue sky and most of all he admired the fact that he wasn't in a yard with guards that had shotguns ready to kill him if necessary. Every bite of the burger tasted like perfection. Every sip of the lemonade was like heaven on earth. Leonard felt like he was back in the high life. He could've sat there all day on that bench and soaked in the area of the Oakland Coliseum. Never before had the Oakland air felt and smelled so good. Leonard threw his trash away and headed back to the bus stop. It was time to begin his new life in his old neighborhood.

Leonard caught the bus from the Oakland Coliseum to the Eastmont Town Center. "Next stop Eastmont Town Center" said the bus driver. Leonard pulled the wire that hung over the seats to alert the driver that he was getting off at that stop. Most people on the bus were listening to music on their Walkmans and CD players. Leonard didn't need any music; the sights of Oakland were like music to his ears. Leonard just wanted to see his beloved Bancroft Avenue (BA as him and his friends called it). Leonard hadn't seen

Bancroft Avenue in 5 years. Bancroft was bittersweet for Leonard. Many of the best and worst times of his teenage years were spent on Bancroft Avenue. BA was the avenue that stretched from The Eastmont Town Center all the way San Leandro (the next city connected to Oakland). BA was known as the street where Black Panthers used to congregate and preach to people back in the late 60's and 70's. It didn't resemble that now. BA was a case study in how a neighborhood can change. The glory days of BA represented unity and family bonding. BA used to represent working class and the idea of Black Nationalism through hard work and success. BA now was famous for having Church's Chicken and a high influx of the gangs that migrated up from Southern California. Leonard hadn't heard much about BA while he was in PSP. The avenue now had some abandoned houses and it wasn't a place you wanted to be after hours. The irony was that during the day Bancroft was a picture of Northern California perfection. Standing in the middle of the block right near Olive Street, you could look up and see the Oakland Hills. The Hills early in the morning were breathtaking. Most people that didn't know the area would ride through BA and think that it was one of the best views that the bay area had to offer. This side of Oakland had picturesque scenery but the underlying tone of East Oakland was dark and evil.

Leonard got off at the Eastmont Town Center and stopped to look down at BA. He could see the corner of 73rd & Bancroft. He immediately got excited and headed towards his sister's house. Leonard was taking it all in and enjoying every moment of the sunny 72-degree day. He noticed every detail of the area. He loved the way the palm trees swayed in the slight breeze. He loved the way the paint was applied on the houses. He was overcome with euphoria by the smell of the chicken coming from Church's. In N Out and Church's were his favorite places to eat. He told himself he would eat Church's later for dinner but had to spread out his love for fast food because of training. He noticed that a few cars rode by and were blasting that same 2pac song. He also heard another car blasting Dr. Dre & Snoop Doggy Dogg. He heard that "Nuthin But a G Thang" song before one of his boxing matches at PSP. Leonard loved being back in Oakland. Although he was apprehensive about being back on the streets of East Oakland, he was ready to enjoy his freedom and start his new life. East Oakland had never looked so good. Compared to the bars and metal of PSP East Oakland looked like Bora Bora. Leonard had promised himself at PSP that once he got back to East Oakland he would work hard and enjoy every day.

Leonard knocked on his sister's door and Alicia answered and gave Leonard a big hug. Alicia showed Leonard his room and it looked like a mansion compared to his former living conditions. Alicia wanted to talk to Leonard about everything he had been through before PSP and at PSP. Leonard just wanted to take a long hot shower and sleep on a real bed. The showers at PSP left Leonard's skin feeling scabby and made him itch. Leonard told Alicia that he would tell her everything after he took a nap. Leonard took a 25-minute shower and washed his body 3 times. He brushed his teeth and washed his face with a nice facial scrub that Alicia had in her shower. The beads in the facial wash made Leonard's face tingle and it felt cleaner than it ever had. Leonard was extra grateful to be with his older sister. He was only thinking of sleeping in a soft bed and opening the window and letting the California bay breeze blow in. Leonard dried off out of the shower slipped on some gym shorts and curled up on the Queen sized bed in his new room. Leonard pulled the comforter over him and laid on both of the pillows on the bed. It took less than 15 minutes for Leonard to fall into a deep sleep.

Leonard slept for over 6 hours. The sun was going down when he woke up. As he left the bedroom and walked into the living room he smelled fried chicken. Alicia had gone to Church's and got a bucket of chicken, corn on the cob, curly fries, and a cold coke. Leonard thanked Alicia and devoured the chicken. Alicia remembered it was his favorite food. She enjoyed watching him eat and was happy that he was doing well and was staying with her.

"Leonard how hard was it at PSP?"

"It was real tough at first but once I joined the boxing team things got easier. PSP isn't the type of place you ever get used to because you can never fully relax there. It was an enlightening experience. PSP was totally different then the juvenile detention center over on Foothills Blvd.”

“Leonard I worried about you but I knew that you would be alright because you’re a tough dude. You were my inspiration even though I couldn’t see you. I knew that if you could survive up there, I could do right out here.”

“Alicia, out here is where it’s at. Behind those prison walls is no place to be. There are a lot of guys up there doing life and never getting out. They have no hope and it shows in the way they act every day.”

“Leonard let me tell you, these streets have changed. The gang violence has taken over and many people have moved further up the bay because of it. East Oakland even made the national news because there was a big shooting on 96th street and some cops were involved. Some dude was blasting “Fuck Tha Police”, the cops told him to turn it down and dude started shooting. Shit was all over the news and the cops had shit on lockdown for a long time. I know you’ll meet up with some of your old crew tomorrow so just be careful.”

“Thanks sis, but I’m not getting into any bullshit. Turning pro in boxing is where I’m headed. I’m done with the streets. I’ll check those dudes out tomorrow.”

“Well we can watch some TV or a movie.”

“Alright let’s check out Boyz N The Hood and then I’m going back to sleep. I love that bed!”

Chapter 17
Wade's,

Morning came and Leonard felt refreshed. He once again took a long shower and smelled a delightful aroma emanating from the kitchen. Leonard peeked in the kitchen and saw Alicia cooking cheese eggs, fried potatoes and turkey bacon. "Damn sis, that shit smells good!"

"Hey L I figured you would enjoy a nice home cooked breakfast."

"Yeah I haven't had one of those in over 5 years."

"Well here you go. L I want to introduce you to my boyfriend today. He comes over a few times a week and also sleeps over. I told him to chill because you came home last night. I think you'll really like him. His name is Byron and he works security at the Coliseum. He can get you tickets to the Raiders game if you wanna go."

'Cool. I'll meet him. As long as he treats you nice we ain't got a problem. If there is an issue then it won't be nice for him."

"Nah L he's cool. We were talking about marriage and a family."

"That's cool. We'll see after I meet him!"

Leonard put on his tennis shoes and headed for E 14th Street. E 14th St is where Wade's boxing gym was. He needed to get a driver's license ASAP so he could stop taking Public transportation. He was thankful for it but was ready to move on and roll whenever he wanted. He walked the 8 blocks up to E 14th St. He wanted to exercise because he missed training yesterday. E 14th St was one of the busiest street in East Oakland. E 14th stretches through a lot of the bay area. It goes from Oakland all the way through San Jose. It had a little bit of everything on it. It has cash checking places, plenty of food trucks (mostly Mexican), Supermarkets, street performers and everything in between. In East Oakland, the strip on E 14th was mainly known as the main center for prostitution in Oakland. Leonard was familiar with that because he had a couple bitches back in '87 that worked a little for him on East 14th. He got into it with a couple of older pimps and had to stop the prostitution game after one of them held a gun to his head and threatened to kill his family. Leonard was fearless but 6 years ago at the age of 16 knew he couldn't go up against the old school pimps from Oakland. Here he was on a new path in life and headed back to E 14th St.

He walked past all of the street vendors and the homeless people. He was trying to embrace being back home without looking out of place. Leonard felt good to be back in fresh air but he was a little scared of all of the options that the streets had to offer. Leonard knew that meeting with Wade was imperative and keeping his career goals was at the forefront of his new life. The fact that he was on parole for the next seven years also wasn't lost on him. He never planned on going back to a life of crime but he knew wrong place wrong time and he was done. Leonard continued his journey from Bancroft to E 14th enjoying his surroundings and focused on getting the gloves back on his hands.

Wade's boxing gym had become a staple in the East Oakland community. Much like the dungeon at PSP, Wade's had the feel of a boxing gym, dirty towels, heavy bags and plenty of sweat. It also had plenty of boxing posters. A couple featured Wade in his first two professional bouts. Many young teenage boys and young men came to Wade's in attempt to stay off the streets. Some had a lot of potential and fought in the State and National Golden Gloves. Others boxed as a way to stay in shape and away from the drug and gang life. Wade, much like CB, was a boxing lifer. He fought as an amateur and a professional. His career was derailed because he was shot during a domestic dispute. He was shot in the right shoulder and his right hip. His boxing career was ended at the age of 25 and he never got the chance to fight for a championship as a professional. He had dreams of fighting on the undercard of an Ali fight. His dreams never materialized but he maintained his love for the sport. Wade was now in his late 50's and lived and breathed boxing. He outright owned the gym and had the apartment above it. Wade realized early on that boxing was all about business. The business was ruthless and boxers could be fucked over quick if they didn't have someone looking over their best interest. Wade went to Laney University in Oakland and got a Bachelor's Degree in sports management. He managed the boxers he trained and had a business attorney that reviewed all the contracts before he or his boxers signed. The boxer was the number one priority for Wade.

He existed for the love of the sport. He was always on the search for new talent and constantly traveled up and down the coast looking for prospects. California had plenty of prospects due to the 5 major cities and also the huge population along with the Mexican Americans that loved boxing. Mexico is a country that loves soccer and boxing! The fighters that crossed the border typically went to San Diego or Los Angeles. Oakland was starting to get an influx of the Mexican boxers and Wade was constantly trying to attract them to his gym. Wade hired several Mexican-American trainers that were bilingual. This helped Wade get some good prospects from Mexico.

"Good morning. May I help you?"

"Yes I'm looking for Wade Taylor."

"Just a moment. What is your name?"

"Leonard Smith."

Wade knew who Leonard was. Once Wade received word that Leonard was doing well in the CPBA he made sure that he attended a few fights. Wade had come to know Conrad over the years through the fights and from a few mutual friends at Patton. Wade respected CB and knew how special Leonard was when he saw him box. Wade knew that Leonard would be showing up, he didn't know when. Conrad wrote Wade a letter to inform him that Leonard would be coming to see him.

Wade entered the room with his signature Kangol on and toothpick in his mouth. "Leonard Smith. CPBA Welterweight champ? I saw you win a fight at Folsom prison in '91, nice to finally meet you!"

"Nice to meet you to Mr. Taylor." Leonard said with pride.

"Leonard, call me Wade. Mr. Taylor is for my father."

"No problem Wade. I'm ready to get the gloves on. It's only been a few days but I feel like it's been a month."

"I hear you. I know you're itching to win on this level and make some real money. Most boxers don't think about their future. Trust me Leonard, boxing is big business. That's why most promoters are former attorneys. They draw up the paperwork and can write language into the contract, which benefits them and fucks over the fighter. I went to college and got a degree in sports management so I could better understand the business of boxing. I also have an attorney that reviews all the contracts for every fighter in the gym. Your best interest is my main concern. Too many boxers are fucked up because of bad management. That won't happen here."

"I don't know shit about the business of boxing. I just want to fight. I'll let you handle that part Wade. I just want to fight for the Welterweight championship of the world. However, I'll learn from you and then when I'm done I'll help the new fighters. When can I get started?"

"You can hang around the gym today. Meet some of the other fighters and I'll review all of the paperwork to get you started as a professional. We are going to schedule your first fight for 3 months from today. I know you have discipline but we need to turn the volume up and teach you more of a pro style. CB did a great job and I'm going to continue to build on what he already established. Let's go meet the guys."

Leonard spent the day meeting all the boxers in the gym and the other trainers. A lot of the trainers heard about him from Wade. Some of the boxers heard of him because they knew guys locked up with him in PSP. Leonard remained humble in meeting everyone. Leonard was truly grateful to be out of prison and for the opportunity to be a part of Wade's gym. Leonard didn't trust many people, but he trusted CB and knew if CB said Wade was fine then he would go with him.

Leonard left Wade's ready to work. Wade was an old Sage just like Conrad. Leonard felt that he could trust Wade but knew that boxing dudes were slimy so he would be on guard. If Wade fucked him, Leonard would hurt him and hurt him bad. That was not at the forefront of Leonard's mind but just like his prison stint and his time on the streets Leonard would keep his guard up. Leonard was due back at Wade's gym tomorrow at 8am. 90 days until his first professional fight. Wade scheduled the fight earlier in the day. Leonard would be fighting a 35-year old veteran Mexican fighter. The guy was tough but wasn't a major threat to beat Leonard. It was a chance for Leonard to have a good pro debut and begin his career with his win. Leonard would train for every fight like it was his last. Motivation for this fight wouldn't be an issue. Leonard wanted to be a rich world champion and have a house and life of his own. Hard work and discipline were drilled into Leonard so he simply had to maintain his focus.

Chapter 18
Transition,

Mutha Fuckin L! Yo I heard you were home dawg. It's good to see you.

"What up T? I got back yesterday. I'm staying at my sister Alicia's crib until I can get something on my own. Been a long time since we've been on this corner."

'Yeah this is our turf now. We control everything that goes on. If mutha fuckas don't pay they taxes then that 187 kicks in. Dig me?"

"I hear you. Pay what you weigh fo sho."

"Damn dawg. A five-year bid at PSP ain't nothing to play with. That time will break the average nigga. How'd you stay up?"

"It was rough. Second day there I had to lay a nigga out. After that I got respect. Joined the boxing team and the next 49 months went by. Cold up that mutha Fucka though. The Bay feels good. Happy to see that Church's and In N Out!"

"Yeah my nig. Your sister told me you got into boxing up there. You always could knock a nigga out. Now you can get paid for it. "

"Yes sir. Just came from Wade Taylor's gym."

"Is that the gym on E 14th?"

"Yeah right near the pool hall. That's where I'll be training."

"I know where that is. Antonio from Fruitvale that used to hang with us in 8th grade trains there. He's supposed to be fighting in the city next week. Don't know if I can make it because Thursday night is money night out here. A lot of dope moving and I have to be around to cash out. L, you need some money? You're always crew thick with me."

"Nah I'm good"

"L it really is good to see you. I'm gonna drop by Alicia's crib later and check on you. Cool?"

"Yeah man slide by and we'll kick it. A lot to catch up on."

"Peace my nig."

"Alright T stay up."

Todd was lucky he didn't get locked up that night when Leonard beat up Patty. Todd's street cred was now off the charts. Street people knew him from the bay all the way down to LA. Todd was bad news and had morphed into the most ruthless dealer in East Oakland. When Leonard last saw Todd, Leonard was the ruthless one and Todd was calmer of the two. Now the roles were reversed and Leonard had something to live for while Todd didn't know if that day would be his last.

Running into Todd brought back some old memories. For a few years at Patton Leonard didn't think much about East Oakland. Conrad told him to always think about what he would do when he got back on the streets. Pressure in a fight was much like peer pressure on the streets. A fighter can be in your face for 36 minutes and hanging with your boys can have you face the same type if pressure. Getting cut off from the social circle is stressful just like a 12 round fight. Conrad knew that prison was probably the safest place for Leonard but knew that he would be released. Now the reality of the street situation was in Leonard's face. He had to rely on his instinct and the discipline that he learned at Patton. Leonard was focused on boxing. Boxing was his main thing. It was all he thought about and all he knew how to do. But what about his old crew? What about Polo? Now that he did 60 months in state, he had time to reflect on all the bullshit that he did back in the 80's. He never apologized to Patty, Todd, Polo, or his sisters. Because of his actions Leonard wasn't allowed to go to Arlene's funeral. That really hurt his sisters because they needed him. He hadn't spoken to Marvin since he told him that Arlene died. There was a lot of unfinished business for Leonard to deal with. He felt he might have to resolve his issues before he started training for the fight because he didn't want any distractions. He needed to prioritize what was most important to him. In his mind speaking to his father was number one and reaching out to Patty Hayes was second. Dealing with Polo and Todd was street shit and he would tap back into that but first and foremost was Marvin Smith his father.

Leonard found out from his sister that Marvin had a one-bedroom apartment over at the Lake. According to Alicia he was now sober and working as a custodian at Lazear Elementary. Leonard expressed to his sister that he needed to resolve his old bullshit before he fought and she agreed. Alicia suggested that he go talk to him at the school. Alicia told Leonard that she would give him a ride over to Lazear. She knew that it was going to be an emotional moment and stayed in the car once they got to the school.

It was after hours so Leonard didn't need to be signed in. He rang the buzzer and Marvin was the one that answered the door. Marvin's face looked like he saw a ghost when he opened the door and Leonard was standing there. Tears and emotion overtook Marvin and he was paralyzed. His feet felt like they were in cement. He literally couldn't move. Leonard saw how emotional his father was and was the first one to speak.

"Hello pop."

"Hello son."

It was the first words they spoke since Leonard found out that his mother died.

"When did you get out?"

"I got out yesterday."

"Where are you staying?"

"I'm staying with Alicia until I get my own place."

"That's good. She checks on me every other day. I got an apartment around the corner. You can stay on the couch if you need to."

"I'm straight; I have my own room at Alicia's. Feels like a mansion compared to that prison cell."

"I bet."

"Your sisters tell me that you were a boxing champ in prison."

"Yeah I was the California prison boxing champ at 150 pounds. I linked up with Wade Taylor yesterday and my 1st fight is in 90 days."

"Yeah I know Wade. He's a great boxing guy. We came up together on the East side. I think he could've beat Ali back in the 60's. I'd like to come to your fight."

"Ok. Pop I learned a lot about life and myself the past 5 years. I know I can't hate you anymore. We haven't talked since you told me mom died. I feel like we really haven't talked since I was 11. There was a counselor at the prison who suggested that I talk to you once I got out. She said I was still mad at you and mom and if I didn't talk to you I would be mad the rest of my life. I didn't want to write a letter. I wanted to talk to you face to face."

"We have a lot to talk about and it will definitely take some time to get through it. When your mom died and I had to tell you, that was the toughest thing I've ever had to do. I felt bad for you. No teenager should have the type of parents that you did. We weren't worth shit to you. You and your sisters deserved better. Kids need the love of their parents and we loved drugs and alcohol. Leonard, please understand that I love all three of my kids. Before I went to the rehab I didn't know how to love. I didn't know how to communicate with y'all. I was angry and mad at your mom and I allowed that to consume me. It affected how I was a father to you. A boy deserves a father. You deserved a father to be there to help guide you through life. I wasn't that. My life was in that bottle. I didn't want to see your mom because she reminded me of how fucked up all of our lives were. I blamed her for being hooked on heroin and not being a mother. I loved that woman with all my heart and she broke it. She chose the drugs over us and that made me choose alcohol. ."

"I know pop, that's what me and the counselor talked about. She told me how addiction worked. I read a book on addiction and we watched a movie in the counseling class."

By this point Marvin was crying his eyes out. All of the emotion he had bottled up the past 23 years was now coming out as he talked to his only son.

"Leonard, please forgive me. Give me a chance to be a real father. You're my only son. I want to make up for lost time. We can't get those years back but we can start today."

"What happened to Mom? I mean how did she get hooked?

"I used to have these card games back in the 60's. It was an all-night party. A lot of alcohol and weed but we didn't do any hard drugs. Your mom wouldn't even come in the card room. She would be looking after your sisters. One night this dude Joey brought his girlfriend over. She talked your mom into trying a little bit, just as a taste. Your mom tried and was hooked for the next 20 years. You never knew who your mom really was. I chased her for 20 years trying to get her back but the heroin had a clutch on her. The old Arlene was beautiful and kind. She could cook, loved her family and treated me like a King. Alicia is just like your mom. All you have to do is look at her."

Marvin made a move and embraced his only son. At this point they were both crying. Leonard told his dad that he forgave him and wanted to move on with their relationship. This was the moment that Marvin longed for. Once he became sober he hoped that he could atone this day to atone for his sins. Leonard wished for the same thing since he didn't have his mother anymore. He needed his father to still school him on manhood. Marvin was now sober and could alert Leonard on the pitfalls of the streets and women. Leonard had already sworn of drugs and alcohol in prison. Training was the way he would get high from now on. Patton was a place he never wanted to visit again. This was a chance for a father and son to build a strong foundation and enjoy manhood together.

"Pop let's have dinner over Alicia's on Sunday. We'll have Yvonne and her family over too. Sound good?"

"Of course! We haven't eaten together since 1982, at least that's what it feels like. I'll be there at 6pm sharp. I'll bring dessert."

"Ok Pop. It was good seeing you. I'll see you on Sunday."

"Can't wait. I love you Leonard."

Leonard was waiting for those words for a long time. He didn't know how to respond. For years he hated both of his parents. He wasn't sure if still loved his dad. But he said it back anyway.

He got back in the car with Alicia and told her about dinner on Sunday. Leonard was quiet during the short drive back to Alicia's house. She knew what he was feeling because she felt it the first time she spoke to Marvin after he got out of the rehab facility. Alicia allowed Marvin to process his feelings without speaking to him. Time in prison gave Leonard the ability to speak to Marvin and forgive him. Leonard was maturing in life, which would help him become a better boxer. Leonard had overcome some major obstacles and he was on the way to turning his life all the way around. Leonard went directly to his room grabbed his pen and paper and began writing an apology letter to Patty Hayes.

Chapter 19
90 Days,

6:00 am and Leonard was up ready to do some roadwork before he hit Wade's gym. Breakfast consisted of 3 raw eggs, 2 bananas and a glass of cold water. Leonard had to maintain his Welterweight frame. He was 5 pounds over the 150-pound Welterweight limit. He wanted to drop the 5 pounds as quickly as possible so in training he could focus on developing a pro style. The CPBA championship wouldn't be recognized on the professional level. Leonard already had a reputation among those in the boxing circle like Wade Taylor. He wrote 90 days on a piece of paper and taped it to the mirror in his bedroom. He also wrote Raul Sanchez, his opponents name next to the 90 days. Just like at Patton, he would use his opponent as his motivating factor for training. CB told him never to take an opponent lightly. Each fight could be your last if you weren't focused. Those words rang in his ear every time he trained. It was a 2-mile run to Wade's and he wanted to do it in less than 15 minutes.

Leonard arrived in a little over 13 minutes. He had his backpack on with all of his training gear in it. He had no idea how Wade implemented his training methods. CB always liked to begin by having the team jump rope. Leonard didn't care how he warmed up, he was just ready to get in the ring and throw his hands up. The fight was 90 days away but Leonard was already laser focused. He didn't need any mental training. All he needed was for the next 2,150 hours to tick away. He was ready to join Sugar Ray, De La Hoya and the other greats and make that real money and stay champion for many years to come but first it started with Raul.

"You get up early, I like that. I'm an old man so I'm up before the roosters. I haven't used an alarm clock in years.

Successful fighters are always up early. Any boxer coming to the gym after 9am, I know they aren't serious about their craft. "

"This has been my life for the past 5 years. I want to be world champion!"

"I believe you will be. Every professional fighter had to start with his first fight. Yours will be here in no time. Once we get past that one, then we'll fight at least 5 more times this year. Since you had all those fights in prison they will count for your amateur experience. 10-0 can get us a title shot. I'll do my part setting the business side up and training you. You hold up your end of the bargain and win that title. Win it for yourself first and second for Mr. Burrell. If it wasn't for him, you wouldn't be in this gym."

"I love and respect CB. I'll never forget what he did for me. He was the father I never had at a time when I really needed him. He guided me through the roughest part of my life."

"I know he did and I know you are forever grateful. Don't worry we'll take care of CB's family and make sure he gets all he needs at Patton. I know CB taught you how to become a defensive wizard. You were sharp at Folsom. You reminded me of Pernell Whittaker. You swim without getting wet. What we're going to work on for the first month of training is the bodywork. Too many guys' headhunt and that don't work because most guys at the professional level can take a punch. But the constant body punches eventually break your opponent down and by the 6th round they are ready to go. You're not going to be able to knock every guy out. Winning on the judge's cards is what we'll focus on. Dedication to the body will allow the knockout to come. "

The first day in Wade's gym was spent watching films of the top welterweights and welterweights from the 60's, 70's, and 80's. Wade commentated the whole time and repeatedly stopped the tape to demonstrate a technique that Leonard could use moving forward. Wade spent all day with Leonard talking boxing and the business of boxing. Leonard was like a sponge. He never paid much attention to the business of boxing at Patton. He saw Conrad talking to managers and promoters who saw him fight but Leonard always let CB handle things. His job was to box and that's what he did.

Wade had that sparkle in his eye when he talked to Leonard. He was waiting for a prized pupil like Leonard to enter his gym. Wade had many good fighters but not a great fighter like Leonard. Wade envisioned the fights in Vegas on HBO. He was more excited than Leonard was. Wade knew what he had. 40 years around boxing gave him a sixth sense on what fighters had talent. He knew how to separate the boys from the men.

"Hey Leonard I have to apologize. I know I can talk. I don't remember getting lunch. How about we head over to Fisherman's Warf and get some dinner and then I'll give you a ride home. It's official training so this is the last bad meal. I have to take you to get the best fish n chips in the state. The next 90 days isn't just about training. It's also about you getting acclimated to life back out here. I know it will be tough but I'll be here with you every step of the way. After tonight take the next two days off. Get your mind right and spend some time with your friends and family. They miss you and need to know you're ok. Monday morning we'll put the gloves on. You can run 6 miles but stay away from the hills. Only flat roadwork."

Wade and his new star pupil headed off for what Wade hoped was the first of many meals together.

Chapter 20

75th,

On a Saturday night back in the 80's there was no doubt where Leonard would be. 75th and Olive is where he and Todd made the street magic happen. They had been like brothers for over a decade. Todd still had love for Leonard. Todd knew that prison could change a man, especially when they go in so young. Todd hadn't changed since '88. He was a few years older but into a lot of the same shit. Difference was now the money was on another level. Todd wanted to head down to LA when he turned 25. Now that Leonard was home he thought maybe they could roll down there together. Todd wanted to put some money in Leonard's pockets. Todd was ruthless but loyal to his people. He considered Leonard to be his closest confidant. In Todd's mind it was time to get the band back together.

"Hey Derrick come here right quick."

"What's up Boss?"

"You know where Leonard's sister Alicia lives?"

"Yeah right down off 96[th.]"

"That's it. Here take this $500 give it to Leonard and tell him to come get at me."

"Alright I'm on it."

Leonard had completed his roadwork for the day and was in his room writing Patty another letter. He felt the first one didn't have everything he wanted to say. He was literally counting down the hours until Monday morning. Wade had bought him a great dinner and they had a great conversation on the ride back from San Francisco. Leonard was starting to warm up to Wade. He believed Wade could take him to the championship. That's all that mattered to Leonard. He was also looking forward to the Smith family Sunday night. Yvonne had two kids and Leonard was excited to meet his niece and nephew. He couldn't have imagined the night he was in the box with detective Ellis that he would again be eating dinner with his father and sisters. Where he was in life hadn't really hit Leonard yet. 72 hours ago he was in a cell with the worst dudes in the state and now he had a soft bed, good food and a new outlook on life.

Leonard heard a knock on the door. Alicia wasn't home so he wasn't sure who it could be. He wasn't messing with any chicks. He cut all of them off when he went to Patton. He looked through the blind and saw Derrick. Derrick was a young cat when Leonard was on the Ave. Leonard always liked Derrick because he was loyal and willing to learn the game the right way. Leonard opened the door.

"Young D what's up dawg?"

"Hey Big L, it's good to see you. Todd wanted me to give this to you. He said come up to 75th and get at him."

"Oh shit this is a grip!"

"Yeah man you know T was going to take care of you."

"That's good looking. D it was good seeing you. Tell T I'll be up in a few."

"Ok. Cool."

Leonard stared at the 5 one hundred dollar bills for a few minutes. He hadn't seen that much money in five years. He was excited. He didn't know what he was going to do with it but he damn sure knew that T owed him that. Detective Ellis tried to get Leonard to flip on Todd. Ellis told him he would shave another year off the deal but Leonard knew that was bullshit plus Todd had nothing to do with it. Leonard had taken heat for Todd before that night so the five hundred was a lifetime payment. It wasn't a biggie to Leonard. The money was cool but T was a brother to him so he was gonna shoot the breeze with him regardless. Wade gave him off until Monday so Leonard told himself he would enjoy his first Saturday night as a free man. He lost five years at Patton. He lost a lot of Saturday nights because of his anger. Tonight would be a celebration for him.

Leonard threw his gear on headed down to 75th. This was like a homecoming for him. He had many mixed feelings about heading back to the scene where he spent many wild teenage nights. 75th was always home. That was the place that took care of him when his own parents didn't. The crew was his family. They went through everything with him. The concrete jungle was his playground. 75th didn't care what time of day or night it was. 75th was an all-night brothel. 75th was like the person telling you that no matter how wrong you were, you would always be accepted.

Leonard's heart was pounding as he approached the corner. He was two blocks away and could see the crew up there doing what they do. Leonard spent many a night lying on his cot in PSP wondering what T and the crew were doing. He daydreamed about the day he could return to 75th. His excitement would bubble over and he would have to shadowbox in order to calm down. As he got closer he heard CB's voice in his head, "the streets are one big pussy waiting to get fucked."

Leonard was an original member of the Ave crew. His first 17 years of existence had been spent right here on this corner. Everything he learned about the hustle was developed right here. He was full of emotion as now he was only a block away. He stopped and looked to his left where he could see the Oakland Hills. The houses were amazing and the view was the best in the bay area. At the top of the Oakland Hills you had a panoramic view of the entire bay area. The big city of San Francisco looked like Gotham city in the batman movies. Leonard envisioned buying a house in the Hills when he became world champion. The view had been there the whole time he just never paid attention to it. Now the Hills were part of his inspiration.

He was an Oaktown boy. Proud to be from Oakland and it was reflected in the Oakland A's hat that he was wearing along with the Raiders T-shirt. Leonard wanted to win the title and have a parade down Bancroft. He thought about buying Marvin and his sister's houses next to him up in the hills. Oakland was his world. Today would his only day to let loose before training started. In a few steps he would once again, for one day, become a member of the Ave crew.

"Welcome back to the Ave! Did you get that deposit?"

"Yeah T good looking."

"You of all people know what it is. We started this thing together. Just cause you went away doesn't mean this spot doesn't belong to you. This is your spot for life. Nobody put in the work that you did. These young cats are loyal but they don't have the juice that you do nor do they have the heart. You are a killer L."

"I hear you man. My killing is going to be done in the ring. I see ain't shit changed. Still out here at high noon like we were."

"You know Noon is the clock in hour. Our job is right here. We've expanded our operation all over the bay. That $500 I gave I you is nothing right now. As soon as you get your License I'm gonna buy you a new whip. You have to train in style. I'm sure old man wants you to run to the gym everyday but when you ain't running you can cruise the bay in a Lexus. Fuck it we'll take the coast down to LA and mess with some of those Compton freaks."

"T you're throwed off man but I appreciate it. So what's up for the day? You still messing with chicks from over the Lake?"

"Man we got chicks all over the bay. You pick where you wanna go and we'll make it happen."

"I need to make something happen tonight because training starts on Monday. You know I'm backed up."

"Yeah cuz nothing but hard dicks the past 5 years. Don't worry we're gonna handle that shit tonight. We'll get a hotel room over by the airport. Do you want to call your cousin down in Hayward?"

"He got a new job and moved to LA. I never wanted him caught up in the streets. His mom was too good for that. His shit was different from ours."

"Got you. Well you know the drill let's head to In N Out but fuck the BART. Let's jump in this '83 Seville I bought."

"This mutha fucka is clean!"

"I have to keep it clean for the bitches. I park it a garage every night and take it to the car wash three times a week. C'mon get in and let's blast this Dr. Dre all the way over to get a grub."

Chapter 21
Saturday Night,

Saturday night in East Oakland is a tricky place to live. During the day it looks like a slice of Americana. Every homeowner has a yard with bright green grass, a palm tree and custom-made ranch style houses. Many have seen the West Coast style houses in the movies. A lot of ranch style houses and Spanish influence on the design of the houses. Riding through the neighborhoods you would think that you were riding through and Oasis for black and Latino middle class. East Oakland didn't have the feel of North Philly or the South Bronx in New York. They were both similar to East Oakland in terms of violence per person. Those East coast cities were filled with tension and people all day every day. In East Oakland people went to work and the streets were empty aside from guys like Todd and Leonard. As tranquil and beautiful as it was during the day it was just as dark and murky at night.

When the sun went away for 10-12 hours, East Oakland went through a transformation. The worst of humanity came out of the streets. Some say you could feel it in the wind when something was going to happen. Gunshots were as regular as fireworks on July 4th. People became immune to the shots. Gangs and drugs were two professions where no pension or 401 K plans were guaranteed. The only thing for certain with that lifestyle was death and prison. The transformation of East Oakland occurred as the sets of young people came out to operate in the darkness. The police set up plenty of tasks forces and were making progress in cleaning up the streets but when you locked one set up another would take its place.

Todd always looked forward to Saturday nights in East Oakland. He felt like he could feel the spirit of the bay running through him. Leonard used to love Saturday nights as well because they would count the money from the week and mess with some bitches. Saturday was the day that the Lord of the streets had granted to them. It was the pinnacle of East Oakland existence. Hustle hard and hustle fast was the motto that the Ave crew adopted throughout the years. Todd wanted nothing more than to have Leonard back in the fold full time.

They spent the day riding through the bay area. After In N Out they headed over to the city and shoot pool. Then they rode down to San Jose so Todd could pick up some money. Leonard saw that Todd was on another level and was moving some major drug weight and making money. Leonard didn't want to be involved in that lifestyle because he never wanted to go back to Patton. Todd was flashing money all day and treating Leonard to everything. Todd was hoping that the money, bitches and cars would seduce Leonard. Leonard was impressed by the material life but he saw how the attraction to the material life got many a cat 25 to life in the state penitentiary. Todd did some time in juvenile detention but had escaped going to a place like Patton so his outlook was different. Leonard didn't want to think too deep on it. He was just happy to be out enjoying the fresh air and hanging with his brother. Todd was just as happy and the eight hours they spent together that day was the best reunion that best friends could ask for. Todd wheeled back to the Ave to count the money. After the money count they were headed to the hotel so Leonard could finally release all of the tension he had in him.

"L come count this money with me. You did that 5-year stretch and never broke. No matter what, this crew can't be broken. Half of this cut tonight is yours. Take the loot and do whatever you want. You earned it."

"My man. Again that's a good look. After this we square though. You out here grinding and I ain't gonna keep taking your profit. I know the game. This will hold me until my first fight."

"Cool. If you need any more before the fight you just let me know. Shit we placing big money bets on all your fights. Let's bring that belt home to the Ave."

Todd was conflicted because as much as he wanted Leonard back on the Ave, he knew that the bid at Patton was tough. Years can change a man. Todd didn't want his friend caught up in any more drama. Leonard had it rough for 23 years. If boxing was his way out then Todd was going to support that. Todd knew that L had calmed down and Todd was upset because he wanted the old days back but was happy that Leonard found something he was good at. Todd was good at hustling and was quitting for anything. He planned on telling Leonard to stay off the streets after tonight. When they left the hotel Todd was going to tell him how much he loved him and to keep his ass in that boxing gym.

"What it look like Derrick?"

"We good. Pulled in $10,000 this week."

"That's what I'm talking about. You split $5000 with the crew and Leonard is getting the other 5. We gotta make sure our champ has the best boxing gear. Fuck De La Hoya! We got our own champ from right here on 75th."

"I'm gonna make ya'll dudes proud."

"My nigga we already proud of you. Ave crew for life! Let's put this shit in the safe house and head over to hotel."

"Let's do it. I need to get this monkey off my back."

"I know you do. We got 2 rooms. So when you're ready to do your thing you got some privacy. These bitches know the deal. They ready to suck and fuck. Told 'em I'll throw 'em a few hundred for coming out to party. I like keeping bitches around so I can call on 'em when I need 'em. They love taking cash and shopping with it. Doesn't matter to me I just need them to do their job. Dig it?"

"Got you."

"Derrick get the crew to help lock up. Nobody will be out here tomorrow. In fact I might head to LA next week so make sure we're good in case the narcs come poking around."

"Yes sir."

Todd and Leonard were right on the corner as they had been many times. It was definitely nostalgia for them to be there together at this time of night. Last Saturday Leonard was in his cell preparing for his release. Leonard would choose 75th over Patton any day of the week. Here he was chilling with the crew and about to get some much needed pussy. As soon as Derrick came back they were gone.

Alicia pulled up on the scene.

"Hey T & L. What's up?"

"Hey there. We're chilling about to head out for the night. What are you doing?"

"I'm headed to the store to get food for dinner tomorrow night. Yvonne and me are going to make a special welcome home dinner for you. T, I want you to come over for dinner. You're the brother that Leonard never had, shit you are his damn brother. "

"Cool. I'll be there. Shit I haven't had a home cooked meal in like forever. I wouldn't miss it for the world."

"I'm gonna grab some Chicken right now too. I'll bring y'all back some to soak up that alcohol."

"Sounds good and thanks Sis."

Alicia pulled off and waved to the guys. Her ford Taurus barely made a sound as she pulled off. Alicia hoped and prayed that Leonard was finally done with the street life. She wanted to get to know him all over again and have him home to help with Marvin. Alicia spent enough time with Marvin to know that he was a changed man and he could finally have a positive influence on Leonard's life. As she drove to the store she smiled and tuned up the song "Gin & Juice" that was blasting from the radio. For the first time in five years Alicia had some peace in her heart and mind and was looking forward to a long awaited family dinner tomorrow night.

Todd could see Derrick taking the money counter into the house. A few minutes and they would be off to the Marriott. The drugs were put in a safe that was partially built into the concrete floor in the basement. Todd made sure that police dogs couldn't find the safe. He sprayed the safe with a dog repellent. Todd was ready to break out as he saw Derrick coming through the living room.

Todd had the keys in his hand ready to give the word to Leonard to hit the car. Todd saw a guy walk up them dressed in gray hoodie wearing boots and a Golden State Warriors hat. Todd couldn't clearly see his face and didn't recognize him by his walk. The crew knew everyone who came on 75th and everyone in the city knew not to come on the corner without permission. Todd didn't think too much of it.

"Leonard and Todd. What's up fellas? Y'all been cool?

Todd replied, "Who are you?"

"I'm P.S. I used to roll with Polo back in the day. We all hung out a couple of times. We had some bitches over by the Lake back in '88."

"I don't recognize your face. Do you remember this cat L?

"Nah I don't either."

"Man we had a ball in '88. Polo said he might pop over tonight. I know how y'all roll on Saturday night."

"Listen man you seem cool but we don't hang with cats we don't know especially on 75th. Ya dig me? So you come back with Polo and we'll kick it. Ok?"

"Yeah man I respect that. I do and I know how it is to protect the turf. If you run into Polo tonight ask him about P.S. and he'll vouch for me."

"No problem. What does P.S. stand for?"

P.S. laughed and said "that nickname is just for tonight." Leonard and Todd looked puzzled. "Just for tonight?" Yeah my real name is Michael Hayes. At that moment Michael reached into his hoodie pocket and pulled out a 9mm.

"Yeah mother fucker P.S. stands for Patty's son." Patty was the lady y'all beat up at the BART in '88. I was waiting for this nigga to get out of Patton." Leonard's heart stopped beating for a moment. He was paralyzed with fear and regret. He wanted to atone for Patty but waited too long. Leonard didn't have a weapon and he knew in this game you were done with no heat. Leonard couldn't even get a word out.

Michael quickly turned and shot Todd in the shoulder. Before Leonard could turn and run Michael hit him in the back of the head with the butt of the gun. & Leonard fell to his knees semi-conscious. At the same time Todd stumbled over to try and help Leonard but fell on the curb. Michael stood over Leonard and without saying another word pumped two bullets into his head. Michael had a silencer on his gun so Derrick couldn't hear the shots. Todd yelled over at Leonard but couldn't do anything to help him. P.S. then stood over Todd. "I'm gonna let you live because I know that piece of shit was the only one that hit my mom but you didn't do shit to help her. That bullet in your shoulder makes us even. You come at me and I'll make sure I kill his whole family and then I'll finish you off. Dig me?" Todd shook his head in acknowledgement. Michael Hayes then disappeared into the Oakland night. Todd didn't even see which way he ran.

The whole confrontation took less than five minutes. Leonard wasn't moving at all. Todd kept yelling his name but Leonard was motionless. Todd started sobbing and inched closer to Leonard. Derrick came running out of the stash house with his gun out but it was too late. Derrick ran up to Todd with a stricken look on his face. Derrick had no idea what the fuck was going on.

"What the fuck happened?"

"This cat was posing like he was a friend of Polo's but he was the son of that chick Leonard beat up back in '88. Check on L and call 911. Hurry up!"

"L wake up. L move your arm. L talk to me baby."

Todd was losing blood and yelled for Derrick to call 911. Derrick ran back to the house and called 911. Leonard had a huge puddle of blood next to his head. Todd looked over and couldn't believe what he was seeing. His best friend for life was dead. Leonard's eyes were wide open and there was no movement from his chest. Todd was starting to lose feeling on his left side and was slipping into a state of unconsciousness.

Alicia pulled up on the scene. Her tires came screeching to a halt. From a block away she could see Leonard and Todd lying in the street. The lamppost illuminated the blood under Leonard's head. She swung her car door open and ran to her brother's side. She let out a blood-curdling scream and lifted Leonard's head into her lap. She rocked back and forth with his head in her lap and blood soaking her clothes. She could not believe what she was seeing. Her car door was still open and the scent of death overpowered the scent of the fried chicken that was on the front seat.

"T what the fuck? How did this happen in 20 minutes? Who the fuck did this? Weren't you strapped? He was supposed to start training on Monday. No! No! No! Leonard wake up baby. Wake up little brother."

"That shit from '88 bounced back tonight. Wasn't shit I could do about it. Dude blended in quick. Started a quick rap and then blasted both of us. I didn't have time to reach for my shit. He spilt my shoulder in half and put two in Leonard's head."

The ambulance arrived and pronounced Leonard DOA. They loaded Leonard and Todd into the same van. A sheet was placed over Leonard's body. Todd was hooked up to an IV and given morphine to numb the pain. His wound was covered with a bandage and they let him know he would survive. Todd tried not to look at Leonard. Todd cried like a baby the entire ride to the hospital. Todd watched as the paramedics removed Leonard's body. They apologized to Todd and wheeled him into the emergency room. Highland hospital was used to seeing gunshot victims. They were prepared to treat and release Todd within 12 hours. Todd's life had now changed forever and Leonard was gone. Todd looked down at the bandages on his shoulder and the tubes coming out of his nose and mouth, and all he could think about what that night at the Coliseum BART. What started out as the best Saturday Night ever turned into the worst Saturday night of their lives.

Chapter 22
Karma,

The sun came up Sunday morning in East Oakland. The smell of Sunday church and breakfast was in the air. Old Grandmothers dressed in their Sunday best were off to praise the lord and tithe their 10%. Marvin Smith was one of the church going people. Since he became sober church was part of his existence. He credited the pastor and members of the congregation for keeping him away from alcohol. The church family was his second family. He leaned on them for everything. He played gospel music as he got dressed for the early service. Andre Crouch was blaring through his 80's Boom box. Marvin still played cassette tapes in favor of the new CD's that the younger crowd listened to. Marvin was especially excited due to the fact that after church they were eating family dinner over Alicia's house. He was grateful to God for the chance to reconcile with his family. Marvin grabbed his jacket and prepared to head out the door when the phone rang.

"Dad."

"Hey Alicia why are you crying?"

"He's gone."

"Take a deep breath baby. Who's gone?"

"Leonard. He got shot last night. Todd too. Todd made it. Leonard died instantly, before his head hit the ground."

"I'll be right over."

Marvin hung up the phone and was paralyzed. Unlike when Arlene died, Marvin was sober and healthy this time. He had a clear mind, body and soul. Marvin understood the depths of what Alicia told him. He also understood what the streets could do. They never sleep and they never forget.

Alicia hung up the phone and sat still for hours. She couldn't believe how much her life had changed in 12 hours. She went from getting food to cook a Sunday family dinner to being the person that the medics asked to identify her little brother's body. She could picture how excited Leonard was to be hanging with Todd and for her going to get chicken for them. She also knew that what Leonard did in the past came back to haunt him. She felt bad because she knew how much Leonard had changed. She saw the growth in him. She saw how much he had changed since he was a teenager. She was looking forward to watching him train to become a world champion. She wanted to be the one to cook him healthy meals and rub his feet at night. It was inconceivable for her not to have her baby brother with her anymore. It was only 3 days since he left the state penitentiary. His life was just turning around and it got snuffed out.

Alicia wasn't under any illusion. She knew that Leonard brutally attacked Patty Hayes back in '88. Alicia thought that the punishment for Leonard was appropriate and was warranted. When Leonard went to Patton she hoped that he would survive and stay alive. If he did that then she prayed that he would be remorseful and rehabilitated. Her prayers were answered because Leonard worked every day in prison to become a better man. She was totally distraught and confused. "Leonard, Leonard, Leonard," is what she said out loud to herself. The rest of their family would be there soon and she would need to pull it together and support their father. Marvin was doing better but still fragile and prone to a relapse. The family couldn't afford any more bad news.

After 4 hours of sitting in the same chair, Alicia walked into Leonard's room. She looked at the pictures on the wall; pictures of Marvin Hearns, Roberto Duran, and Sugar Ray Leonard. She looked at his boxing shoes and his gloves. His bag from prison was sitting on the floor. She saw all the letters that were exchanged between Leonard and friends and family. She saw a picture of Conrad Burrell. The autobiography of Malcolm X was in the bag along with the release letter from the California Board of prisons. The program from his first prison fight was in there too. Alicia got an even better picture of how Leonard spent his time in prison. She smiled as she saw his GED certificate. It continued to make her extremely sad as she saw the man that Leonard was becoming. The teenager that stirred up shit all night on 75th was gone and replaced by a young man that aspired to be world champion of the world in the Welterweight division. He would now never realize that dream. CB wouldn't see the fruit of his labor pay off. Alicia remained sad and nostalgic as she closed the bag. She looked on the dresser and saw a letter addressed to Patty Hayes. She opened the non-sealed envelope and saw a letter that Leonard had written to Patty. Alicia sat on the bed and began reading it.

Chapter 23
The Letter,

Dear Mrs. Patty Hayes,

This is Leonard Smith the young man that attacked you at the Coliseum BART back in 1988. I never apologized to you because I never had the chance. I took the plea deal, which meant neither courtroom nor trial. I wasn't sure if I would survive in prison. I'm glad I did because it gives me a chance to say I'm sorry for what happened 5.5 years ago. There is no way to take it back and believe me I wish I could. When I saw you get on the BART it triggered something in me that I didn't know was there. You look a lot like my mom. The night I saw you on the BART my mom had just died less than 24 hours prior. I had been drinking malt liquor all day before I got on the BART. I told my boys I wanted to get something to eat but I really wanted to beat somebody up. It was you Mrs. Hayes. Every night for 5 years I wished that you hadn't gotten on the BART. I wished that you got on after the Coliseum. We were going to In N Out at the Coliseum. You did and I made you pay for everything that Arlene Smith did to me. Mrs. Hayes my mom was a heroin addict. I was neglected almost from birth. During elementary school I had to eat leftover food from friends during lunch. I often wore the same pair of shoes for years even though they were 2-3 sizes too small. My father didn't help much because he was an alcoholic. He would come from work, give my oldest sister some money to buy groceries and then go to the bar. During my teenage years all I wanted was for my mother to come home from work and cook a nice dinner for us. It would've been awesome for my mom to come to school and look at what I was working on. Maybe volunteer to be the mom who was responsible for giving my 2nd grade teacher a Christmas gift. Mrs. Hayes I'm sure you are that type of mom. When I saw you on the

BART I envisioned that you did all of those things. I pictured you tucking in your kids when they were in 1st grade. I pictured you staying up with them and helping them make cookies or helping them with an arts and crafts project. There is no excuse for doing what I did to do you at the Coliseum that night. I did 5.5 years in Patton for that crime. Patton is the worst prison in the state. It was no place for a 17-year-old kid but it was what I deserved. I deserved more years than that. I'm glad that I spent time there. It gave me a chance to reflect on who I was and what I did. I went to counseling classes in order develop a conscious. Early at my stay at Patton I didn't understand the depth of what I did to you. I was still angry with Arlene and as far as I was concerned you represented all that she wasn't. Words can't make up for what I did to you. I know that but I would like for you understand how remorseful I am. I'm not the same guy I was when I saw you that night on the bus. I don't mean to repeat myself but its how I feel. I started and stopped writing this letter at least 10 times. I wanted to make sure it reflected how sorry I am. I finally decided to just write from the heart and not worry if it was perfect. Life was miserable for me. It is totally unfortunate that I saw you on the worst night of my life. I will forever be linked to you because a night won't go by where I won't think of you. When my head hits the pillow I'll think of you and hope that you're ok. Detective Ellis told me the extent of your injuries. I know the hospital bills must've been a lot. I took up boxing in prison and won the CPBA championship. I am going to continue my career on Monday morning at Wade Taylor's gym. I would like to pay all your medical bills in full. If you already paid them I would like to give you the money. In prison I thought how it would be if I could apologize to you in person. I learned that a major part of my rehabilitation is to meet with my victim face to face. Maybe we can get to that level. I don't expect you to ever forgive me but I need you to look in my eyes and see how sorry I am for what I did to you. It's important that I look you in the face and apologize for treating you the way I should've treated my mother. I was still hoping that she would get clean and become a mother and a wife. She never did. I missed her funeral. When they put her in the ground I was on the way to Patton. If I was on the street I'm not sure if I would've gone to her funeral. My family *would've begged me to go but I hated her. She made my life hell and at the time I was glad she was dead. I saw my dad earlier for the first time since I got sent to prison. He's doing very well. He went to rehab and seems to have kicked his alcohol addiction. He tried to be a dad but he was also in pain because of my mother. As you can tell she caused a lot of pain for our family. I'm looking forward to building a relationship with him. Mrs. Hayes you're alive which means there is hope for me to make it right. You changed my life. If our paths hadn't intersected I might've been dead by now. The desire to better myself came from a violent act I committed at your expense. I plan on doing whatever I can to make it up to you. I hope that you can receive this letter in the spirit in which it was written. Mrs. Hayes I sincerely apologize for attacking you at the Coliseum BART on July 12th 1988. Please accept this letter as the first of many attempts to make it right between us.*

Sincerely,
Leonard Smith

Alicia saw that the letter was dated November 5th, 1993. She thought, "Leonard wrote this letter this morning." The emotion was more than she could handle. Leonard really did make a 100% turnaround. That letter showed that he was ready to move forward and atone for all of his past sins. He would never get that chance. How would Marvin get past this? All Marvin talked about was reconciliation with his only son. In rehab he would speak to Yvonne and Alicia for hours about all of the things he wanted to say to his son. Marvin wouldn't get that chance. Wade and Conrad would never get the opportunity to see their star pupil manifest his destiny and become world champion. Leonard would never get to fight for that world championship. He wouldn't get the chance to go back to Patton and build a new gym for Conrad. He wouldn't get the chance to talk Todd into leaving the streets alone and become part of his boxing entourage. Leonard Smith was dead as a result of bad decision-making and a shitty upbringing.

The morgue had already put a tag on his toe and placed him in the freezer. They were waiting on the family to let them know which funeral home would be handling the body. The medics gave Alicia the $5000 cash that he had in his pocket. She would use that for the burial. Alicia closed the bedroom door. She left the letter Leonard wrote on the dresser. She knew that the cycle of violence wasn't going to end. Todd would eventually kill Michael and whomever Michael rolled with would be looking to kill Todd. Alicia didn't want anything to do with it. She was already planning to move. The memories of Leonard and her family pain were too much to bear. Atlanta was sounding like a great move.

<h1 style="text-align:center">Chapter 24</h1>

<h2 style="text-align:center">Lessons,</h2>

Payback comes in many forms. This time it came back in the form of a young son seeking retribution for the beating of an innocent woman who happened to be his mom. No one in the Smith family had any idea that Michael Hayes existed. Innocence can never be overstated. Leonard took that from Patty and Michael made sure that he wasn't going to take that from another mother. Who's to blame? Michael? Arlene? Todd? There was no answer for that question. Leonard was a product of a horrible situation. He could've made better decisions, he chose not to. Everyone close to Leonard agreed that he needed help to become a better young man. Conrad stepped in and played the role that Marvin never did. It was too late for any of the questions surrounding Leonard to be answered.

If the story of Leonard Smith were a movie the credits would be rolling. It would show Alicia contemplating and pondering her existence in Oakland. It would show Yvonne consoling Marvin in his apartment. It would show Todd back on the corner with his arm in a harness, speaking with Derrick about finding and killing P.S. It would show Wade at Patton visiting with Conrad and telling him about Leonard's death. The Arial camera shot would fade out and show the corner of 75th & Olive Street in East Oakland, California. That corner represented the life and times of a young man that was full of potential. We'll never know if Leonard would've been champion. We'll never know if the redemption story was truly complete. What we do know is that Leonard was a tortured soul that made a fateful decision that he could never outlive.